MAGIC REVEALED

Dragon's Gift: The Seeker Book 3

Linsey Hall

DEDICATION

To Claire, my best adventure buddy. Without you, I'd have far less cool stuff to write about.

CHAPTER ONE

Deep in the Honduran Jungle

"Those vultures can't be a good sign," Nix murmured from behind me.

"Yeah. They know something we don't." I glanced up as I pushed my paddle through the muddy brown river. Vultures circled above us, black spots on the patch of blue sky visible through the gap in the jungle canopy.

Sticky sweat rolled down my back as I turned my gaze back to the wide river. The jungle crept in on either side, a brilliant green death trap. The scent of foliage, water, and mud was so strong that it drowned out the stink of my sweat.

Slightly behind me, Nix manned her own paddle.

"The vultures must mean we're close," she said. "We've been going for at least three hours. And my dragon sense is really starting to buzz."

"Mine, too." The treasure we sought was near. I'd read all about it in an old treatise I'd found in the back of my trove, which had given my dragon sense just enough of a clue to work. "And the magic is getting stronger."

"No kidding," Nix muttered.

The jungle's magic buzzed along my skin, prickling like gnat bites. The farther we pressed on, the stronger it became—protecting the treasure we sought. The long-abandoned hidden city deep in the Honduran jungle had been built by supernaturals. Which meant there'd be some serious booby traps.

My ears strained as I searched the river and forest ahead. On either side of us, massive green leaves rustled in the faint breeze. The jungle was thick, the sounds of birds and monkeys like an out-of-tune chorus. Through the greenery, I caught sight of a flash of black. It appeared again a moment later, keeping pace with our boat.

I squinted into the jungle. The black glinted in a ray of light. Fur. Sleek, black fur. And a big yellow eye.

"We've got company." I paddled faster. "A jaguar is stalking us."

"Great," Nix muttered. "Vultures and jaguars. The next thing we need is a giant snake."

"Careful, or we'll get one." I knocked on my head, hoping to ward off the jinx.

Mountains loomed ahead, steep green peaks jutting up into the cloudless sky. My muscles tensed, awareness of surrounding threats keeping me on a tightrope.

"My money's on the city being in the valley ahead," I said.

"Not taking that bet," Nix said. "I think you're right."

Thirty minutes later, the river had carried us deep into the mountains and we could see glimpses of white ahead.

"That's it!" Nix cried.

We drifted down the sluggish river, mountains hulking over us like silent sentinels on either side. In front of us on the left side of the river, an abandoned city spread across the jungle. Small white buildings—houses, maybe— popped up between the foliage. The vultures overhead had tripled in number, and the jaguar stalking us still popped up now and again alongside.

Magic prickled fiercely against my skin. A warning.

"Stay alert," I said. "Something's coming."

As soon as the words left my lips, the water ahead of us exploded in a massive splash, drenching us. I sputtered, heart pounding, and barely managed to keep my grip on my paddle.

I blinked the water out of my eyes, only to see a huge snake rising high in front of us, its beady black eyes riveted to our boat. I nearly swallowed my tongue, my gaze glued to the long white fangs protruding down from its mouth. Pearlescent poison dripped from the tips.

"Crap!" Nix cried.

The bottom half of the snake disappeared under the murky water. I couldn't see, but the thing had to be at least fifty feet long given the size of the part I could see. Magic rolled off the snake, thick and pungent. Smelled like a freaking swamp.

"A booby trap to protect the city," I said.

In a flash, Nix's magic swelled on the air behind me, the scent of flowers strong. I followed suit, calling on my magic and letting the icy cold fill me as I started to shift to my Phantom form.

Before I could change, the snake struck, its huge head shooting toward us. I swung my paddle up and struck it in the eye. The thing hissed and reared back.

As the snake shook its head, I chucked the paddle into the boat and shifted fully, letting the ice fill my limbs as they turned transparent blue. My heart thundered as I reached out and drew my sword from the ether, the slender blade appearing from thin air. Fates, I loved that trick. This new sword was amazing.

Nix stepped closer to me, holding a massive spear that she must have conjured.

"I'll—"

The snake struck, cutting her off. She thrust the spear up, piercing it high on its body. The thing hissed, and for the briefest second, it held still, stuck on the spear. I leapt up, turning corporeal long enough to slice my blade through the snake's head. The massive thing dropped off, blood spraying me on the face and shoulder. I gagged as the head dropped into the water with a splash.

The huge body collapsed, yanking the spear from Nix's hands. The splash that followed rocked our little boat, throwing me to my butt. Pain seared through my hip where I fell hard against the wooden bench, but I kept my grip on my sword. Nix landed beside me as water splashed over us.

"Not bad," she said breathlessly.

"Nah." I struggled to my feet, gazing out at the rippling water and trying to wipe the blood from my face. "I just hope there was only one."

"We can handle another." Nix stood and dusted off her hands. She strained and pointed to her face. Then to her head and shoulder. Finally, she gestured to her whole body. "You've got a little something there."

"You don't look so good yourself." The spray had gotten her, too, speckling her brown hair and pale skin with red flecks. Her green eyes stood out starkly, an exact match to the blue T-shirt she wore.

Nix stuck her tongue out in a gagging gesture. I returned my sword to the ether, then bent and scooped up some water, trying to get the worst of the blood off my face. Nix followed suit.

Once we were less gross, I said, "The spear was a good idea."

Nix bowed low, grinning. "You did exactly as I'd hoped."

I high-fived her, then looked up at the vultures circling overhead. "I bet they're disappointed."

"I'm cool with that."

But the birds didn't leave, which couldn't be good.

I picked up my oar, then turned to shore. The city spread out before us, beckoning. The jungle had long since reclaimed the side streets, growing rampant around the buildings. But the avenue in the middle was still mostly clear. Perhaps a spell.

We paddled to shore, beaching our small boat at the edge of the river and climbing out. Mud squelched under my boots as I climbed onto firmer ground.

"Now what?" Nix asked.

"That way." I pointed down the main avenue through town. A massive pile of white stone rubble lay at the other end.

Nix didn't normally come treasure hunting with me, but she'd wanted to get out of the shop. I also had a feeling that Roarke had asked her to watch my back. My sorta-boyfriend/Warden of the Underworld was off dealing with some problem on his home turf in hell, so for the first time in two weeks, he wasn't glued to my side.

Nix scuffed her foot over the packed-dirt road, which was firm despite the recent rains. "Has to be a spell."

"Yeah." Supernaturals had used all kinds of magic to keep the city looking nice.

Magic prickled on the air as we set off down the street. On either side, white limestone houses stood empty. They stretched all the way toward the mountains behind. A monkey peered out from the window to our left, chattering at us.

I waved at him, then continued on.

Pain lanced through my skull as a blue light flashed in my eyes. I stumbled, blinded, and crashed to my knees. For the briefest second, the blue flash brought with it a sense of familiarity. Then it vanished.

"Del!"

Woozy, I blinked, struggling to my feet.

Nix gripped my arms, her concerned gaze glued to my face. "What the hell was that? Are you okay?"

"Yeah, yeah. Fine." I looked left and right, checking for danger, but the only threat was coming from within my own head.

"What was that? A seizure?"

"No. I don't know what it was. It happened last night, too, right as I got in bed."

"Why the heck didn't you tell me?"

"Didn't seem like a problem." I shrugged out of her grip. "We gotta get going."

"Yeah, sure. But if that happens again, tell someone. It can't be normal."

I laughed. "Nothing about us is normal."

"True." Her grin turned serious. "But there's quirky not normal and *you need a brain scan* not normal. So if it happens again, tell someone."

"Yeah, yeah, Mom. Let's go." But she was right. There was something weird about that blue light. Once might be a fluke. Twice…

"Get a move on," I said.

She punched me in the shoulder, then turned and started down the street.

We walked for another five minutes before we reached the end of the street.

"Oooh, that's not good," Nix murmured.

The destroyed temple loomed in front of us. "Sure isn't."

A wide moat stretched out before us, dotted in a hundred places with small slabs of stone. Prickly magic emanated from the pond, indicating some kind of protective spell. It surrounded a massive pile of rubble that had once been this society's high temple. Like most supernatural temples the world over, this temple had once contained enchanted artifacts. The problem with enchanted artifacts was that the magic within them decayed over time. Once it reached the tipping point—boom.

"Definitely not good," I muttered. "We'll have to cross using the stepping stones. But there are so many that I bet you have to step on certain ones if you don't want trouble."

"This isn't the kind of trouble I'm interested in."

"Same." I studied the moat, unable to figure out a pattern, then glanced at her. "Any ideas?"

"Nope."

"Then let's hope for the best." Gingerly, I poked the nearest stone with the toe of my boot. When it held firm, I stepped on it. My muscles relaxed slightly when the thing didn't sink, but tension still tightened my skin. I'd never walked on a frozen lake, but I'd bet it felt something like this.

"Follow me," I said. "And if shit goes south, get out of here."

Nix laughed. "Like I'd leave you."

Slowly, we made our way across several stones. The fifth stone I stepped on vibrated the moment my toe touched it. Before I could pull back, the thing exploded, throwing me backward. I surged toward Nix, stumbling. She grabbed me, but not before my boot dipped into the moat. The rubber sole sizzled and melted.

"Shit!" I yanked my foot up, balancing with Nix on one stone, and bent my knee to peer at the sole of my shoe. The rubber had been eaten away almost to my sock. At most, there was a sliver left.

"The moat is full of acid." Nix's voice wavered.

"Yeah." I tightened my arm around her waist as my skin chilled. "I don't even want to think about what that would do to skin."

"Eat it. Immediately."

I swallowed hard, then jumped when a growl ripped through the air.

No.

Slowly, I turned my head. A jaguar crouched on the shore ten feet away, its gaze riveted to us.

"Oh, hell." Nix's arms tightened on my waist.

Trapped. We couldn't go back to shore or we'd become Kitty Chow, and we couldn't go forward because we didn't know which stone would explode and chuck us into acid.

"He looks hungry," Nix said.

"He looks like he's never tasted human before, but has heard good things and is interested in trying it."

Nix choked on a laugh before her gaze turned serious. "Turn into a Phantom. He can't hurt you in that form, and maybe you can kill him."

I flinched as the jaguar prowled forward. "I'd really rather not kill him."

He was beautiful, ravenous yellow gaze and all. I really didn't like killing animals. My *deirfiúr* Cass had once run into demon jaguars. It was okay to kill those, since they were technically demon shifters. But this guy was just a giant cat.

"Niiice kitty," Nix murmured.

The jaguar growled.

"Shhh! He doesn't like that." I could draw my sword to be on the safe side, but I had a feeling he wouldn't like that either.

Out of the corner of my eye, I caught sight of a dusty footprint on a stone to the left. It was so pale that I hadn't seen it from shore.

"I've got an idea," I said. "Conjure a steak. A big one."

"Okay." Nix's magic swelled as she unwrapped an arm from my waist. A moment later, a raw steak appeared in her hand. It had to weigh at least ten pounds.

The big cat's yellow gaze snapped to it.

"Toss it to him," I said. "Then conjure another."

Nix tossed the steak. It landed with a *thud* on the ground next to the jaguar. He scooped it up in his jaws and chomped on it.

"You're a handsome guy," I said. "Smart, too, I bet."

His gaze met mine like he understood me as his white teeth tore into the meat. I might've liked him, but I couldn't help but imagine what it would feel like to have those fangs chomp into me.

When he swallowed the steak, Nix tossed him another. It went down the hatch faster than the first.

"Is that your preferred cut?" I asked the cat. He didn't respond, but I felt like maybe he smiled. Not that I believed he could speak English, but maybe he liked my tone.

"Another," I said.

"'Kay." Her magic swelled, and she tossed another steak at the cat.

This one, he ate slower.

"I think he's getting full," I said.

"Good. I don't want to burn through all my magic." She eyed the cat's fangs as they tore through the steak. "Although, it's for a worthy cause."

Once the jaguar had finished the third steak, it looked at us with a satisfied expression. At least, I assumed it was a satisfied expression. I thought its belly was looking a little fatter, and fates knew I was always satisfied when my belly was full.

I pointed to the pile of ruins on the other side, then looked at the jaguar. "Can you lead us there?"

The cat just stared, yellow gaze impassive.

"Can you take us across? There will be more steak." I felt crazy for assuming the cat understood, but I'd always had an affinity for animals, and I had to try. Maybe I'd get dumb lucky.

The cat stood, then stalked over to the left about ten feet. Right near the dusty footprint.

"It understands!" Was I getting better at communicating with animals? I swore I could feel a connection with the big cat.

"I can't believe this might work," Nix said.

"Let's try."

We hopped back across the stones to the shore, then followed the jaguar across the path that he took. My heart was lodged in my throat the whole time, but eventually, we made it to the other shore.

"Oh, fates," Nix said when she stepped onto solid ground. "I can't believe that worked."

"Me neither."

The jaguar turned to us expectantly.

"But you'd better conjure another steak and pay up."

"No kidding." Nix did her thing and tossed a steak the jaguar's way.

He leapt up and caught it in the air, then found himself a spot on a stone ledge and lounged with his prize in the sun, completely ignoring us.

My shoulders relaxed as I turned to face the temple. It was nothing but white rubble stacked in piles, destroyed long ago by the blast of decayed magic. There were a few short walls still standing, but not many. Flowers bloomed among the ruins, some kind of bright pink jungle blossom that I couldn't identify.

"Shame it was destroyed." Nix bent and picked up a hunk of stone that was carved like a monkey's face.

"Not for long." It was part of our new plan for our shop, Ancient Magic. To date, we only collected and sold magic from artifacts that were extremely decayed and about to blow.

But with my new power, why not try to collect magic from artifacts that had already self-destructed? All I had to do was bring the artifact back from the past. The bonus was that we could restore the temple to its former glory if we removed the destructive magic from the original artifact. With the magic gone, the artifact wouldn't blow up and destroy the whole site. We'd bring back a piece of history. In a place as remote as this, no one would know who had done it.

Of course we wouldn't bring the people back, since that was bound to be trouble. I wasn't even sure what would happen if I tried to bring people back—it probably violated some kind of natural law.

"Let's go." I set off, weaving through the piles of rubble. "We need to find that giant monkey."

According to the ancient treatise I'd read, this place was known as The City of the Monkey God, and a massive monkey statue had once held a place of honor in the temple. I'd bet my luckiest necklace that the monkey was the decayed artifact that had blown this place to bits after it had been abandoned.

"It's pretty," Nix said as we climbed over rubble covered in flowers.

Birds chirped in the distance, an ever-present jungle soundtrack. At one point, a monkey darted out and poked me.

"Haven't seen people ever, I'd guess," Nix said.

"Yeah." I focused on my dragon sense, letting it tug me through the destroyed temple. It was a faint feeling, but strong enough to follow. A few minutes later, I stopped. "I think we're here."

"Yeah?" Nix looked around. "Looks the same as everything else."

It did. Just piles of stone scattered here and there. "It was a doozy of an enchantment if it caused this much damage when it finally went *boom*."

Nix stepped back. "I'll just let you do your thing."

"Thanks."

The size of the place sent a niggling sense of doubt through me. Could I really bring back something this huge? And to the right time? The doubt was familiar, but I quashed it. I now had control of my magic. I could do this. It might not feel familiar to trust myself, but I was going to make it feel familiar.

Practice, practice, practice.

I sucked in a deep breath and closed my eyes, envisioning this place as it might have once been. I didn't have a lot to go on. There had been no illustrations in my book, just a brief mention by a historian that an ancient culture had lived in a city deep in the Honduran jungle. They'd died out or abandoned the place around the turn of the first millennium. Sometime later, the magic in the monkey statue had decayed fully and exploded.

Magic thrummed beneath my skin, coalescing to form an orb of light in my mind. I used it to feel the history in this place and bring it back.

Sweat broke out on my skin as I pushed my magic, giving it everything. Though I had control of it now, it was still like a muscle, and I hadn't worked out. Exhaustion trembled through my limbs as I worked, keeping ahold of my magic and molding it to my will.

"Whoa." Nix's quiet exclamation made me open my eyes.

The familiar blue glow spread out from me, reaching across the floor. Piles of rubble disassembled and rolled upward, forming walls. Stone animal heads that had broken off long ago returned to their rightful bodies. The place rebuilt itself, piece by piece, creating a massive room that was fit to worship any god.

My heart leapt. I'd done it!

In the center, a huge stone statue grew.

"The monkey," Nix said.

I grinned as I let my magic flow, feeding the statue and bringing it back to life. The final result was over twenty feet tall, expertly carved and brimming with magic. In front of it, the air shimmered, roughly human shaped.

"Del!" Nix pointed to it.

Shoot. I pulled back on my magic, careful not to go too far. Last thing I wanted to do was bring back any living beings. The shimmer in the air faded, leaving just us and the monkey. Light streamed in from gaps in the wall near the ceiling, shedding light on the massive space.

Nix walked in a circle around the monkey. "This thing is bigger than I expected."

"No kidding."

"We're going to have to change the procedure. Put the magic in something smaller."

"Yeah. I'm not interested in trying to haul a replica of this guy out of here." Normally, Nix took the magic from the original artifact and put it into an identical replica she'd conjured. This was not normal.

"How about a mini monkey?" she asked.

"Perfect." I stepped back and pulled out my cellphone, then began to snap pictures of the monkey statue and the surrounding temple, keeping my ears perked for the sound of approaching footsteps. I'd brought this place back to a period when it should be abandoned—approximately 100 years after the last recorded habitation—but you just never knew.

Near the monkey, Nix set to work. This was her specialty. When we'd set up our shop, she had learned how to magically forge the artifacts Cass and I found so that we could put the originals back in their resting places. It kept our consciences clean and us on the right side of the law. Normally, she'd do it at the shop, but she'd been ready to get out from behind the desk.

Her magic swelled around her, the scent of flowers delicate on the air. She knelt and pressed her right hand to the monkey's leg, then hovered her other hand over the ground. When she closed her eyes, the hum of magic grew.

Her left hand glowed. Beneath it, a small monkey statue began to materialize. A moment later, it appeared fully—a perfect replica.

"Now for the next step," she murmured.

She bit her lip in concentration as magic flowed from the large monkey statue to Nix's hand in the form of blue smoke. It hovered around her palm. Once she had gathered it all, she let it sit for a moment. She'd told me once that she infused it with a bit of her own magic to stabilize it a bit. Once the magic stopped shimmering and looked like simple blue smoke, she moved her hand to hover over the miniature replica and pushed it into the stone. Once it had disappeared into the replica, she picked it up and stood.

"Done!" She displayed the monkey. "The magic won't last forever, but it's stable enough that we should be able sell it and the buyer will have time to use it."

"Good enough for me." I spun in a circle, checking out the now intact temple. "And this place can now rest safe."

With the dangerous magic now removed from the giant monkey statue, we'd changed a tiny bit of history.

The magic would never blow up the monkey statue or the temple. We'd brought this place back from the dead.

"For a while at least."

"Yeah." Time would always win. This place would break down naturally as all ancient places did, but not anytime soon now that the monkey's magic had been taken out of the equation.

Nix tucked the monkey into the pocket of her cargo pants and approached me. "You know, this wasn't so hard. I don't know why you and Cass always come back all bloodied and stuff."

I groaned. "Jinx us, why don't you?"

She laughed, the sound echoing in the massive chamber.

I knocked on my head for good measure and turned for the exit. We didn't have any transportation charms, and like most magical cities, this one was protected against people just transporting in via magic. So the only way out was the same way we'd come in.

We hurried across the temple. The air in the temple was cool and the light dim. Stepping out into the sweltering brightness of the mid-day jungle was a shock to the senses. I blinked against the light, then gasped.

The courtyard all around us had returned from the past, just like the temple, and it was spectacular. I hadn't realized my magic had traveled this far. The ground was paved in white limestone. Statues of animals and humans lined the walkway toward the moat.

"Nice," Nix said.

Magic prickled on the air, and it wasn't ours.

"Yeah." My heart pounded. "You might want to conjure a weapon. I don't know what kind of protective enchantments I brought back."

"Oh, hell." Her magic swelled slightly, and a moment later, a bow appeared in her hand. A quiver full of arrows materialized at her back. "You can't just send this place back in time and get rid of whatever protective enchantments might try to get us?"

I shook my head. "Not now that we've taken the magic from the statue. We changed history. The temple compound was technically never destroyed because we took the magic that decayed and exploded."

I eyed the statues warily as I stepped out of the temple.

The stone beneath my feet shot into the air, carrying me up with it. I stifled a scream. The statues weren't the problem. The ground was.

"Jump!" Nix yelled.

I was at least eight feet in the air and rising. I leapt off, not wanting to find out how high this thing would take me. I stumbled when I hit the ground, going to my knees. Before I could rise, the stone I crouched on lifted into the air, taking me with it. I scrambled off. Every stone I walked on tried to carry me off, so I sprinted for it, leaping from stone to stone as they rose into the air.

"Come on!" I cried.

I could hear Nix behind me as we sprinted across the shifting ground. My breath heaved as I raced, my lungs burning. We'd made it halfway to the moat by the time the ground stopped moving. I skidded to a halt, panting.

"Oh, fates." I panted, leaning over to prop my elbows on my knees.

Nix did the same.

Somewhere nearby, stone scraped against stone. I shot up in time to see a monkey statue come to life, rising up on two feet. It was easily ten feet tall.

"*Now* these things want to party?" I returned my sword to the ether, since it would do a fat lot of good against stone, and adopted my Phantom form.

The monkey clambered toward me, too fast for a thousand-pound statue, as far as I was concerned. I called upon my new ice power, letting the chill flow through me. When it had filled my limbs, making them heavy and cold, I threw out my hands and directed an icy blast at the ground in front of the monkey's feet. Ice formed in front of him. When his massive foot hit the gleaming stuff, he slipped, crashing to his back.

"Nice!" Nix said.

Behind the monkey, a jaguar statue and a huge stone snake came to life. Their heads turned toward us, then they charged.

"Oh, hell," I muttered. They were all enchanted, not just the monkey. "I don't have enough power to defeat them all. We gotta run for it."

"Yep!" Nix spun and sprinted toward the moat.

I followed, turning occasionally to shoot ice at the statues' feet. They slipped and fell, but more kept coming. Another stone monkey darted out from my left side, swiping a massive paw through my Phantom form.

I shot ice at his feet and he slipped, crashing to the ground. When we reached the moat, we raced for the special stones.

"Which ones?!" Nix cried.

"To your left."

She spotted the right one and leapt across. I followed, praying they still worked. My heart stayed lodged in my throat the entire time, but we made it to the other shore safely. When I turned to look back at the temple compound, all looked normal and quiet. The statues had returned to their proper places. My ice glittered in places, but that would melt soon.

"Whew." Nix panted. "The spell died."

"Yeah." I propped my hands on my hips. "It looks so danged normal, you'd think we were freaking out for no reason."

On the other side, the jaguar lounged, half his steak uneaten and his gaze on us. The expression on his face very clearly said, *Overreact much, ladies?*

One minute, you're about to die, the next, a freaking cat is making fun of you. Life.

I stuck my tongue out at him, then turned to Nix. "What do you say we get back? I think I need a bath."

"Yeah, you and me both, dude."

CHAPTER TWO

By the time Nix and I arrived back in Magic's Bend, we were dragging. Exhaustion was a monkey on my back— one of those stone monkeys we'd narrowly escaped back in Honduras.

But that didn't mean we were sleeping. Oh no. It was party time.

I showered quickly, switched out my lucky bracelet for a lucky necklace made of fae silver, then grabbed my keys and hurried out of the apartment and down the stairs. By the time I stepped out onto Factory Row, the sun had set fully and the night was brisk. I shivered and zipped my leather jacket up to my neck, then turned left and headed to Potions & Pastilles.

Lights spilled out from the windows, illuminating the sidewalk out front with a golden glow. I pulled open the glass door and stepped into the warmth of the coffee shop. In honor of the occasion, the interior was done up in twinkle lights and balloons.

My friends had pushed the tables aside and were gathered in the middle of the room. Cass, Aidan, Nix, and Claire stood around the birthday guy, Emile. Connor, resident music expert, was in the corner fiddling with the sound system.

"Del!" Cass cried. "You're back."

"Yep!" I grinned as I approached. "Mission accomplished."

"Nix was telling me." Cass nudged Nix with her shoulder. "Not bad, all in all, huh? With your new power, the sky's the limit in terms of the artifacts we can recover."

It was a big responsibility, and normally that might have given me hives, but warmth filled me at the idea. I turned to Emile, the man of the hour. He was a skinny guy with dark hair and a kind face. A black and white rat sat on either shoulder, each wearing a tiny paper party hat that matched Emile's. Emile was an Animus mage, and Ralph and Rufus were his buddies.

"Happy birthday, Emile!" I said.

He grinned. "Thanks."

I scratched Ralph under the chin, then Rufus.

"They like you," Emile said.

"I like them." More than most humans, really. And it seemed that my connection to them was possibly growing.

Claire hiked a thumb toward the bar and grinned, her dark hair gleaming under the twinkle lights. "Help yourself. There's a box on the counter."

"You know me so well." I headed toward the counter, grateful for my awesome friends.

I was fiddling with the spout on the box of red wine when Cass approached, silver can of PBR in her hand.

"So, when will Roarke show up?" she asked.

"Not sure. Once he's done with the problem in the Underworld. Some minor demon uprising."

"Those common?" Cass asked.

"I think so? I really need to ask more about it." Roarke and I had known each other only a couple weeks. He wasn't technically my boyfriend, but he was the closest thing I had to one.

I finally got the little tab of silver foil off the wine box spout. "Jackpot!"

"Any luck with your dragon sense and finding Draka?" Cass asked as I poured wine into the coffee mug I'd snagged from behind the counter.

My shoulders slumped slightly. "No."

I'd been trying every day—every hour, almost—to get a hint of Draka's location, but my dragon sense was too weak. Like always.

I tried to shake off the crappy feeling of failure. Moping would do no good. And it was possible that she was blocked from me somehow, which scared me more than anything.

Concern darkened Cass's eyes. "You really think something has happened to her?"

I leaned against the counter and clutched my wine. "Yeah. I mean, I don't know her well. Just through my dreams and the few times she helped me a couple weeks ago—but why the heck would she just disappear like that? She came to me as soon as she escaped the

Underworld and helped me when I was in a bind. Then, nothing. Zip. Nada. She's gone. And I'm really worried."

Cass squeezed my shoulder, and I leaned into her touch, but it did little to banish the chill of concern that iced my skin. I just had this *feeling*. And for someone as superstitious as me, that meant something.

"You know we'll do whatever we can to help, right?" Cass said.

"Yeah, I know." I just needed to do more. It was my responsibility.

As I raised the coffee mug to my lips, the blue light flashed in my eyes again. My grip loosened on the cup, and it crashed to the counter, shattering. I staggered, my eyes blind. Cass's grip saved me from cracking my chin on the counter.

I panted, blinking to clear my vision as Cass helped me stay on my feet. My knees felt like jelly.

"What the hell was that?" she demanded.

"Again!?" Nix cried.

Cass's head whipped toward Nix. "What do you mean, *again*?"

"She did this before! Back in Honduras. And last night."

Cass glared at me. "Why didn't you say anything?"

"I didn't think it was anything!" I rubbed my forehead, trying to dispel the ache that had set up between my eyes like a troll crouching under a bridge. "Apparently I was wrong."

"What do you think it is?" Nix asked.

Behind her, everyone else had gathered, their concerned gazes glued to me. The front door opened, and Aerdeca and Mordaca stepped inside, looking like light and dark in their usual outfits of icy business woman and Elvira, respectively.

Great. Just what I needed. More people to witness my descent into madness. At least Roarke wasn't here.

"Well?" Cass demanded. "What do you think it is?"

"I honestly don't know." I sighed. "But it's getting stronger. And…and more familiar." It felt crazy to say it, but it *did* feel familiar. "I don't think it's bad."

"Hmmmm." Skepticism flashed on Nix's face, her brows drawing close and lips pursing.

Ralph and Rufus hopped off Emile's shoulders and landed on the counter, then ran across and jumped onto me. They scaled the sleeves of my jacket, perched on my shoulder, and rubbed their little faces against my neck. Warmth filled my chest.

"Thanks, guys." I stroked each on the back, then met the gazes of everyone staring at me. "Just give me some space, okay? I'll figure it out."

Everyone frowned, even Aerdeca and Mordaca, both of whom usually appeared aloof regardless of the circumstance.

I stared everyone down, and eventually the party started up again. Despite the drinks and music—curated by Connor, of course—there was a heaviness to the air. Like something was about to happen.

I collapsed into bed and slept like the dead.

Except for the dreams. Because of course I wouldn't get a break. I almost didn't even realize I was dreaming, except that I'd banished this place from my memories long ago.

But I was back there in my mind. Back where it was dark and cold. Darker and colder than any other place I'd ever been.

Damp stone, hard beneath my butt and back as I huddled against the wall of the cell. By memory, my gaze was trained on the place where the door was located. Not because I had any hope of escaping—there was no hope of escaping the Monster's dungeon—but because I longed to see light when it finally opened.

Unlike my two fellow prisoners and only friends, I wasn't afraid of the door opening, no matter how bad it was on the other side. I could be the one they dragged away next, but I didn't care. I was so desperate to see light that I'd take the risk that they'd choose me next.

"How long have we been here?" whispered the girl next to me.

I'd only ever caught glimpses of her face in the flash of light from the door. Enough to know that she had pale skin and red hair and was roughly my age. I was about fourteen, I thought. That was the last birthday I remembered. Draka had been the only one there. My chest ached to see her again.

I reached for the girl's skinny hand and gripped it tight. "I don't know."

"We'll get out," said another girl. Her fingers closed around my other hand.

She had brown hair. I tried to picture her face as I'd seen it in a brief flash of light, but that was all I could remember.

"But how do we escape?" I asked. However long I'd been in here, the time had stolen my hope of getting out.

"I don't know," she said. "But we'll do it together."

I squeezed her hand tight. Her words gave me a flicker of hope. No matter what happened, we were together. I wasn't alone.

I leaned my head back against the stone wall and stared up at the dark ceiling.

I dozed off, as I often did. It was my only escape.

At first, I thought the flash of blue light was my imagination. But when the familiar sense of warmth and the smell of sweetness struck me, my heart raced. The air swirled with a blue glow.

Draka!

My friends whimpered and drew back, but I leapt up and raced into the middle the small cell. The blue glow coalesced to form Draka's dragon form. She wrapped her shining wings around me. Warmth and comfort surged through me, driving out the hunger and cold. We had a connection, Draka and I, forged by some magic I didn't understand. She was always there for me. My true family.

"I'm here to take you home," she said in my mind.

The ether tugged at me. Draka began to spin around me as a blue haze, igniting her magic. Pulling me away from my friends!

"No!" I cried. "I can't leave them. They must come."

"I cannot," Draka said. "I am not strong enough."

The ether pulled harder as Draka tried to use her magic to pull me away. I could've escaped! Gone home! Though the idea of escape made my heart sing, home was a much more frightening concept.

But it was better than this nightmare.

"Don't hurt her!" one of my friends cried.

It snapped me back to reality.

"I can't leave them!" I resisted Draka's pull. I didn't know where I was or how to get back to save my friends. And I couldn't leave them here—not after all we'd been through. We were a team. I wouldn't abandon them.

"Come back when you can save us all," I begged.

"I cannot." Sorrow echoed in Draka's voice. "You must come now."

I fought her, unwilling to abandon my friends. When the door to the cell burst open, blinding light flashed into the dark room. The guards shouted, throwing something toward us. Light burst again, this time from some sort of weapon. My skin stung wherever a fine mist hit it.

Draka hissed and disappeared.

No!

I jerked upright in bed, gasping. Tears streamed down my face, and sweat stuck my hair to my neck. The memory of the dream made my heart pound like an elephant's galloping footsteps.

With a shaky hand, I pushed the hair off my forehead and glanced at the clock. Seven in the morning.

I groaned and let my head thump back against the headboard. Pain shot through my skull and I winced.

I was a mess.

I climbed out of bed on trembling legs and dragged myself to the shower. The hot water blasted away some of the shakes that made me feel like a noodle, but my mind was still racing by the time I got out and dried myself off.

I pulled the fluffy robe off the back of the bathroom door and tugged it on. It was covered in little cartoons of dancing seals, but the familiar sight didn't make me smile as usual. I'd just stepped out into the living room when a knock sounded at the door.

I frowned. It was way too early for Cass or Nix to be up.

"Who is it?" I called. No one else had access to the green door that led up to our apartments.

"Roarke." His deep voice carried easily through the wood.

My heart leapt, and I hurried to the door and yanked it open. Who'd let him in? Probably Cass or Nix.

Roarke stood on the other side, two paper coffee cups and a paper bag in his hand. He grinned, so handsome in his black jacket that my head swam a little.

Mentally, I kicked myself. I *really* needed to get it together. Twenty-five years of not losing my head over a dude had given me weak resistance muscles. Ever since I'd decided I trusted Roarke—which wasn't that long ago, in fairness—I'd been a freaking ninny about him.

"Hey." My gaze roved from his dark hair down to the boots on his feet, taking in the height and muscles that made my blood race every time I saw him. We'd only ever kissed and shared a couple of exhausted, chaste nights in the same bed, so my stupid hormones were in overdrive.

This guy was making me act like a teenage boy.

He raised his brows. "Can I come in?"

"Uh, yeah." I stepped back awkwardly, realizing that I'd been staring at him for who knew how long.

But hell, I wasn't going to kick myself over it. After that shitty dream, I'd take whatever distraction I could get and be grateful for it.

Roarke stepped in and set his stuff on the table, then turned to me and pulled me close. My heart jumped as he leaned down and pressed his lips to mine.

His kiss was firm and soft all at the same time, so perfect that my heart raced, and I had to grip his shirt to keep my balance. The sandalwood scent of his magic swirled with the fragrance of the soap he used, making my head spin.

He pulled away and leaned his forehead against mine. "I found that I missed you while I was gone."

A smile tugged at my lips. "I missed you, too."

And I had. More than I'd expected. Whatever was between us was casual. At least, it should've been.

Maybe it wasn't.

Roarke pulled away, and his gaze met mine. Concern turned his dark eyes fully black. "Are you all right? You look a bit pale. I didn't think my kissing was that bad."

"Oh, it's not." I scrubbed a hand over my face. "Just a dream. I'll be better with some coffee. Is one of those for me?" I pointed to the cups on the table.

He picked up the smaller one and handed it over. "Double shot of espresso. Motor fuel."

"Thank you." I took the cup gratefully and sipped, sighing at the familiar taste of Connor's perfect concoction.

I reached for Roarke's hand, then pulled him to the couch. He sat and I curled up next to him, close enough that my side was pressed against his. The contact made awareness prickle across my skin.

"Did you just finish up in the Underworld?" I asked. "All demon uprisings repressed?"

Wearily, he dragged a hand through his hair. "It may have been a false alarm. I couldn't find anything when I reached the supposed location of the troubles."

"Hmmm. That can't be good."

"It's unusual, to say the least." He took a big sip of his coffee, then looked at me. "Are you sure you're all right? That must have been a terrible dream."

"It was." I polished off the last of my espresso, then reached for his hand. His strength gave me strength. And I wanted to talk about this. I had to.

"Do you remember how I told you about being held prisoner as a kid by a guy we called the Monster?" I asked.

"I do. Did you dream of it?"

"Yeah. I've never actually remembered what went on in that cell while we were held prisoner. It's lost with all my other memories of the time before I woke in that field ten years ago. Cass has remembered some stuff, though. Like how he wanted us for our FireSoul powers and that we attacked a guard and eventually escaped. But last night, I dreamt of it for the first time. Draka tried to save me."

"She did?"

I nodded, worrying my lip. "But I wouldn't let her take me without Nix and Cass. When the guards came, they drove her away. The weird thing was—when she told me she was taking me home, I was afraid."

"Of her?"

"No. She always makes me feel loved. It was the idea of home that was bad." I frowned. "But then, all my memories of home haven't been great."

Roarke tugged me to his side and squeezed. I leaned my head against his shoulder and tried to absorb his warmth.

When Cass had recovered her memory, she'd learned that she'd had loving parents who'd died trying to save us from the Monster. But everything I was learning about my past made my heart feel like it was full of lead.

Suck it up. Plenty of people had crappy childhoods. I was here, wasn't I? Happy and healthy, with friends and a great life.

I wasn't going to let this crap drag me down. Draka needed me.

Which meant I needed to get back to trying to find her. However I could.

I patted Roarke's thigh. "Thanks for listening. I'm going to go get changed."

I stood and headed for the bedroom. As soon as I stepped over the threshold, pain tore into my mind, followed by a flash of blue light that was so bright I went immediately blind. My legs turned to jello and I fell, crashing to the ground on my hands and knees. But even they wouldn't hold me. I collapsed to my front.

The pain receded almost immediately, leaving behind the most familiar feeling of comfort and warmth. And that memorable sweet smell.

Draka.

My dragon sense roared, latching on to her.

"Del!" Roarke's voice echoed through my mind, like he was yelling from the other side of a football field.

I blinked, trying to push myself up off the floor. But I couldn't budge. I was a noodle once again, and this time, I was about as lifeless as one. I felt Roarke's strong hands as he rolled me over gently, then picked me up. He cradled me against his chest as my vision began to clear. He was walking. Taking me to the bedroom.

"I'm okay," I croaked. I rubbed my forehead, which now only ached slightly.

"You don't look okay." He reached the bed and was about to set me on it.

I pushed at his chest. "No, set me on my feet. I'm not an invalid. I'm fine."

Better than fine. I was great.

Roarke put me on my feet, and I clung to him, waiting for my legs to remember their job. The blue light had shocked my system, sending it into a tailspin.

"Draka contacted me," I said. "I know where she is."

"What? Just now?"

I nodded, grinning. "Yeah. The last couple of days, I've been seeing this flash of blue light. I didn't know what it was. But it was her. It happened again just now, but this one was a real doozy. It's like she finally succeeded in reaching me."

To his credit, he didn't look at me like I was nuts. He also didn't let go of my arms, clearly afraid I would face-plant. I probably would.

"What did she say?" he asked.

"Nothing. She didn't have to. We have a connection." A memory from my dream flashed in my mind. I'd thought the same thing when she'd come to save me from the Monster's dungeon. Now it was my turn to save her.

"What does that mean?"

"I don't know, really. I think the connection was broken when I lost my memory. But it's back, and she gave me a clue about her location. A place for my dragon sense to find."

"That's great. Where is she?"

"Close. Surprisingly close. Only a couple hours away." I pushed away from him and wobbled over to my dresser, gaining strength with every step. I turned back to him and made a shooing motion. "Scram. I need to change. We have to leave immediately."

"You're not well enough. You're walking like you just spent a year at sea."

I turned. "I don't care. She's my family. I'm going to get her. Now." I tested out a few small jumps, keeping my jello-legged wobbling to a minimum. "See? I'm almost back to normal. You can't stop me, Roarke. Not when it comes to saving someone I love."

Resignation sliced across his face. He nodded, his gaze solemn. "I get it. We just need to play it safe. I don't want anything to happen to you."

A small smile tugged at the corner of my mouth, but my mind was totally preoccupied with what it might take to save Draka. I couldn't fail. I just couldn't.

CHAPTER THREE

I didn't even knock on my *deirfiúrs'* doors to let them know we were going. Nix had to man the shop, and Cass was supposed to head off on a big hunt today. And we'd partied hard last night, stumbling home together well after midnight. They'd be totally knocked out.

I'd send them a text when I knew more. I needed to learn what we were up against before I brought in the big guns. Most rescue missions required stealth, not numbers.

So Roarke and I hurried out of my apartment after I'd changed and loaded up with lucky amulets from my trove. I wore a lucky T-shirt, two lucky necklaces and an assortment of bangles that had been enchanted by a sorceress in India. As usual now, my sword was stored in the ether instead of sheathed at my back.

I didn't look like it, but I was dressed for war.

"I'll drive," Roarke said as we stepped out into the brisk morning air.

I gazed longingly at Scooter, wanting to race off toward wherever Draka was sending me, but Roarke was right. We both needed to get there, and as big as my Harley was, it wouldn't fit him. Not easily, at least.

"Okay." I followed him across the street to his sleek electric sports car. Birds chirped their little heads off, clearly oblivious to the huge thing that was happening.

Finally, I might be able to find Draka. I'd been dying to see her since she'd delivered the news that I was a Guardian. And I'd been growing ever more worried with every day that I hadn't seen her.

We climbed in, and Roarke shot away from the curb, then asked, "Where to?"

"North. Out of town. Get on Magician's Way, and it'll take you out of town."

He made record time through the quiet streets of Magic's Bend. Since it was Saturday morning, it was a ghost town, even in the Historic District. The brunch places wouldn't start bustling until at least ten. The highway was quiet as we made our way north. I did my damnedest to keep my legs from bouncing like I'd had ten Red Bulls.

"Nervous?" Roarke asked.

"Yeah." I gazed out at the trees that raced by. "I just want this to work, you know? I've been so worried."

He reached over and squeezed my thigh. I knew the gesture was meant to be comforting, but it just made my blood race. I barely resisted whipping my head toward him.

He removed his hand quickly, gripping the steering wheel tight. Apparently the move had backfired on him, too. Comfort was all well and good, but when there was as much amazing sexual tension as we had, *any* kind of touch could turn racy.

I dragged my thoughts away from Roarke and focused on my dragon sense. It pulled northward, but we were getting close.

"Do you know what we'll find at the other end of this hunch?" Roarke asked.

"It's not a hunch. And no, I've got no idea." I hoped it was Draka and that she wasn't in trouble.

My mind raced as we drove. I directed Roarke off the highway, leading us onto a small road that delved deep into the woods. Eventually, huge trees appeared. Glittering white snow covered the ground between the redwoods.

"Impressive," Roarke murmured.

Massive trees loomed on either side of the road, so big that you could carve a tunnel through them to make a road fit for cars. I leaned low, trying to see to the tops of the trees nearest my window, but failed. There were no other cars on the road this deep into the woods.

Without warning, my dragon sense lit up like a pinball machine. "Stop!"

Roarke slowed the car, pulled over to the side of the road, and cut the engine. "Here?"

"Yeah." I climbed out, my boots crunching into the snow, and zipped my jacket against the chill air. All around, redwoods rose like silent sentinels. Thousands of years old and hundreds of feet tall, my mind almost couldn't comprehend them. There were no smaller trees or bushes. Just giant trees and snow. I'd never seen anything like it.

Roarke's door shut quietly, and he came around to stand next to me.

"I'd heard these were here, but never made a point to visit." His voice was low, awed.

"Same," I whispered, my head tilted back all the way so I could see the tops of the trees. They were like skyscrapers.

I spun in a circle and tried to absorb the magnitude of the place. The snow gave it an even more enchanted air. I could stand here forever, just soaking in the wonder.

But that wouldn't save Draka.

"There's nothing out here except trees," Roarke said. "Which way to Draka?"

"Come on." I followed my dragon sense away from the car, cutting between the massive trees. It was silent all around, the animals all battened down in their burrows, avoiding the cold. The trees were endless in all directions, and the sun sparkled through the branches far above, making the snow beneath my feet glitter.

I tried not to be swayed by the grandeur of the place as I walked, doing my best to stay on high alert. I really had no freaking idea what to expect.

When an oddly small tree to my left shifted, I jumped. Roarke threw out an arm and stopped my forward movement. I stared hard at the tree, which was only about eight feet tall. A baby—no, a fetus—compared to the monster-sized trees all around.

In the blink of an eye, light swirled around the tree, and it burst to life, hopping out of the ground, roots and all. It turned, facing us. With its face.

The tree had a freaking face, about three quarters of the way up the trunk. The branches were leafless and moved down like arms, bending in front of the tree so that it could take a bow.

"What are you?" I demanded.

The tree straightened. "That's quite rude."

Shocked, I blurted, "I'm sorry."

I'd never had a tree call me rude before.

"You should be." It looked between Roarke and me, its barky face creasing with annoyance. "And now you should turn around and leave."

"No."

"Out of the question," Roarke said.

"You are not permitted past this point." The tree indicated a line in front of itself with a branch.

But Draka was past that point. I knew it. "We have to cross. My friend needs us."

"I assure you, your friend is not here."

Fat lot that he knew. I stepped left, intending to inch around him. "I just have to check."

"No!" Blue light swirled around the tree's branches. The scent of its magic welled in the air—green leaves and dirt.

I did *not* want to find out what that magic did.

Instinctually, I threw out my hands, sending my ice magic at the tree and envisioning a dome. As I'd hoped, blue-tinged ice grew up from the ground, forming a thick dome over the tree. The blue magic shot from the tree's branches, slamming into the ice. The ice didn't so much as crack.

"Quick thinking," Roarke said.

"Yeah." I admired my handiwork and the tree within, surprised I'd accomplished something like that. I hadn't even taken the time to doubt myself, which was probably a good way to go about things.

"Rude!" shouted the tree. "You'll regret this!"

"Will it be all right?" Roarke asked.

"Yeah." I grabbed his hand and tugged him around the ice dome. "But we better get out of here before the dome melts. He doesn't look pleased."

We hurried away. I glanced over my shoulder to see the tree glaring at us through its icy prison. *Yikes.*

The feel of magic in the air increased as we walked. I was about to draw my sword when the ground exploded in front of me. Snow and dirt flew as a massive root burst out of the earth. It whipped toward me, wrapping around my waist like a thick lasso and hoisting me up into the air.

Shit!

Blood rushed to my head as it flipped me upside down. The forest floor was at least forty feet below. I strained, twisting in my cage and trying to find Roarke.

He hung upside down as well, gripped by the tree to my left. My gaze traveled up the massive trunk, three hundred feet into the air. At least I didn't see a face on that redwood.

A tornado of gray light swirled around Roarke. His gray demon form appeared. The root holding him exploded as he burst free, using his massive strength to break the cage that held him.

He plummeted for only a second before flipping in the air and shooting upward toward me. From the look in his eyes, he was going to break me out the same way he had himself. But I didn't want to hurt the massive tree.

It wasn't the best idea, in terms of self-preservation, but these things were damned majestic and thousands of years old. They were like the archaeological sites of the tree world. And weren't roots like super important for survival and all that?

They needed those roots.

"Don't!" I cried as he neared. "Don't hurt the tree. Hover below me and catch me, okay?"

His gaze snapped to mine as the tree's root shook me like a baby with a rattle. Or Godzilla with what's-her-name. Either way, it sucked.

"Just do it!" I cried.

He nodded sharply and darted down, waiting just below where the tree held me. I called on my Phantom magic, letting the icy chill flow through me. My limbs turned blue and transparent, and a moment later, I fell from the massive root's grip.

Wind tore through my hair, and my stomach jumped. Roarke caught me, clutching me close and zooming off, his massive wings carrying us between the trees. He darted around roots as they popped out of the ground and snapped toward us.

A moment later, I realized that he hadn't even flinched when he'd caught me. Was he immune to the

Phantom magic that made most people miserable when I touched them?

It seemed so.

I didn't have time to dwell on it. Roarke turned left, dodging a hefty root that burst out of the ground, and my dragon sense protested.

"Go back!" I cried. "To the right."

He whirled on the air, dodging the root, and followed my directions. He flew so fast that my hair whipped in the wind and my eyes watered. I clung to him, grateful that he was a little bit warm in the icy wind. We passed a dozen more trees before the roots finally stopped breaking out of the ground and attacking.

"We can go down now," I said.

Roarke nodded and drifted to the forest floor. His boots crunched in the snow, and he set me down. My skin chilled as soon as I lost his warmth.

"Aren't you cold?" I nodded at his chest. Magic had removed his shirt when he'd shifted. Wings didn't exactly fit in the average human-shaped shirt, after all.

"It's not bad," he said. "I'll stay like this. Who knows what's coming next."

"Well, you got us out of that one, so I'll take the next," I said.

"You handled the mini tree."

"Not as impressive as you taking on a forest of giant redwoods."

"Not really. The blue magic that small tree was about to throw was a powerful memory loss charm. I recognized the signature. It would have blown our minds away, and we'd have spent eternity wandering the forest with no idea where we were."

I swallowed hard. *Shoot.*

Talk about scary.

"Then we're even," I said. "We just see what the next challenge brings."

I turned and led him through the forest, trying to keep my senses alert. It was hard not to be awed senseless by the majesty of the giant trees, but the memory of the ones with enchanted roots kept me on track.

"Whatever we're going for, it's well protected," I said.

"That's what has me worried. Why would she send you to such a dangerous place?"

He had a point. Problem was, I didn't know the answer. So I kept my mouth shut and shrugged. The forest grew ever more silent and ever more magical as we walked. The snow glittered white and pure, and flakes began to tumble from the sky.

"I think we're getting close." My dragon sense was really starting to roar.

A half second later, I slammed into an invisible wall, bouncing back and falling on my butt.

"Del!" Roarke knelt by my side. "Are you all right?"

"Just a moron." My face and chest ached from where I'd slammed into the barrier. I rubbed my nose gingerly, grateful to feel that it wasn't broken. "You'd think I'd learn, you know? I ran into one of these things just two weeks ago."

Roarke held out his hand toward the barrier, no doubt feeling for the magical signature. He turned back to me. "In fairness, it's a well-made barrier. Barely a hint of magic."

I sure hadn't felt the warning prickle that normally accompanied enchantments like that one.

Roarke stood and offered a hand. I grabbed it, and he hoisted me up.

"Think you can break this one?" I asked.

"Not a problem." He turned to the invisible wall. His magic filled the air—the scent of sandalwood and the taste of wine. I sucked it in, unable to stop myself from enjoying it as he drew back a fist and slammed it into the air. His fist plowed through, and a hundred tiny white cracks appeared in the air, radiating out from the blow.

I reached out, and my hand passed through. "Good job."

Together, we stepped through the barrier.

And right up to a wall of fire. Heat blazed, singeing my face.

Panic flared briefly before I threw out a hand and blasted a wall of ice at the flames. Roarke and I stumbled back as the blue ice grew and engulfed the orange flames, killing them.

"Bloody hell." Roarke dragged a hand through his hair.

All I could do was pant, adrenaline making my limbs shake, as I stared at the charred line on the forest floor where the flames had once been.

"That was quick thinking," Roarke said.

"Yeah." My voice was whisper-soft. "That was a really good backup protection. Was it hidden from sight?"

"Yeah, an illusion charm, I think. Once we broke the barrier and stepped through, we could see it."

"Geez." I looked around at the forest.

Besides the scar on the ground where the flames had once been, it was as quiet and pristine as before. Majestic trees stood witness to our near-barbequing. "I thought that castles and dungeons were the real scary places. But this forest is nuts."

"That's the truth."

"We're close. Really, this time."

"Just stay on the alert," Roarke said. "We may make a good team, but this forest has had some serious tricks up its sleeve."

Team. I liked that.

I shook away the thought. Roarke and I were… I didn't know what we were. But now wasn't the time to start wondering or to get all sappy about it. We had a deadly forest to survive.

"This way." I set off, following my dragon sense.

When we reached the clearing, I pulled up short. Ahead, there was a precise circle of redwoods.

Surrounding nothing.

"We're here," I said.

Roarke met my gaze, skepticism on his face. "Really?"

"I know. It's weird. There's nothing there."

"Not that we can see."

"That's what I'm afraid of."

He laughed. "Let's take a look."

We explored the clearing, which was roughly half the size of a football field. When I found nothing interesting, I went to the middle and began scraping at the snow with my boot. If ancient sites had taught me anything, it was that if there wasn't something above ground, there was something below it.

The snow was only about four inches deep, so it was easy to move. Ground gave way to gray stone, so I scraped off more snow from the rocky area.

"Give me a hand!" I called to Roarke.

He came over and helped, his bigger feet and longer legs making quick work. We made our way in a circle, revealing one large, flat round stone. We were careful not to step on it.

"What do you think it is?" Roarke asked.

"I don't know. I've only ever seen one similar, and it was a portal."

"Portal?"

"Yeah. Let's try it out."

I went to step on it, but he held out a hand to block me. Before I could dart around, he stepped onto the stone with both feet, not giving me a second to get a word in edgewise.

Nothing happened.

"Not a portal," he said. "I feel no magic here."

"You jerk. You jumped me."

"I knew you'd hop on."

I scowled, stepped onto the stone next to him, and poked him in the chest, ready to deliver a lecture.

But the ether pulled at me immediately, sucking me into the blackness of space. My head swam, and my heart raced.

A moment later, I was spit out into another forest. It had smaller trees and no snow, but it was no less magical.

Behind me, Roarke said, "Where are we?"

I spun, taking in my surroundings. The trees were thick with bright green leaves, and violets bloomed at their bases. In the distance, a burbling brook provided a lovely accompaniment to the chirping birds. It had a very Enchanted Glen feel to it.

And the weather was entirely different. A balmy seventy degrees that was toasty compared to the redwood forest.

"It feels familiar," I said. "There was only one other place that felt like this, and it was accessed by the same type of portal, but it's—"

A deep growl sounded from behind us. I whirled, but Roarke pushed me behind him protectively.

Annoyance surged as I darted out from behind him to get a look at what was coming. He flared out a wing to keep me from going closer, but I peered over the top of the gray feathers. I caught the briefest glimpse of fiery eyes peering out from between the leaves of a full bush before a massive beast leapt out at us.

The huge dog pulled up short when its gaze locked with mine.

The growl died, and the dog's lips pulled back in what I could only assume was a doggy smile. But it was no normal dog. It was nearly the size of a horse and jet black. The fire in its eyes had died—and when I said fire,

I meant literal flames—and they were now a glittering black. The lolling pink tongue was the only color on the animal's whole body. The scent of brimstone rolled off of it.

"A hellhound," I said. But not Pond Flower. She was brown and white, and I'd know her anywhere.

"You trust it?" Roarke didn't lower his wing from where it held me back, but that didn't stop the dog. It trotted toward us.

"Yeah. I know this hellhound." I darted around Roarke's wing.

He—or she, I couldn't tell—stopped right in front of me and gave my arm one long lick. It was a thank you lick. I didn't know how I knew, but I did.

Leaves rustled from behind the dog, and other hellhounds popped out. Five of them.

Roarke stiffened. "Get back."

"No. Seriously, I know these dogs."

They trotted up, their happy gazes riveted to me. Each one gave me a good lick, and while I appreciated the sentiment, that much hellhound spit got gross after a while.

"They sure like you," Roarke said.

"Yeah. I saved them from a pretty crappy owner. But we didn't have room for thirteen hellhounds, so we sent them here."

He turned toward me, brows raised. "Thirteen?"

"Yeah. The others must be somewhere else." I met the first dog's eyes. "Will you take us to the fortress?"

The hellhound nodded, then turned and trotted off toward the sound of the river.

"You'd better shift." I pointed to his wings. "You look a bit threatening, and our hosts won't appreciate it."

He nodded. A swirl of gray light gave way to his normal form, now dressed in the same sweater he'd been wearing earlier.

"Who are our hosts? Where are we?" he asked as we followed the small horde of dogs.

"We're in the Arcadian forest. It's at a waypoint, a magical place between here and nowhere, and it's the home to the League of FireSouls." I'd known it felt familiar. Cass, Nix, and I had come here a couple months ago, though we'd entered through another portal and ended up in a different part of the forest. "Why would Draka be here?"

"What is the League of FireSouls?"

"Cass calls it a magical justice league, and that's basically what it is. A group of FireSouls that's been around for hundreds of years, though members rotate. They aren't immortal. Their goal is to protect our kind from persecution. But because we're still targets, their base is located here."

He glanced around. "It's well hidden, I'll give it that."

"Exactly. But I have no idea why Draka would be here. She's part of my Phantom side, not my FireSoul side."

"Are you sure she's here?"

"I thought she was, but now that we're close, I don't feel her." That didn't mean she wasn't here, but I was starting to doubt. I called on my dragon sense and it pulled hard toward the FireSoul's fortress. "She definitely wants us here, though."

A rustling sounded from up ahead. A brown and white hellhound burst through the trees, charging us with her tongue flying out the side of her mouth.

"Pond Flower!" I knelt and she collided with me, painting my face with kisses. I laughed. "Gross! Quit it."

"This one is your favorite, I take it," Roarke said.

"Shhhh. Don't say it where the others can hear." I stood and ruffled the fur on her head.

She turned and we followed, headed toward headquarters, tail wagging high in the air.

"For some reason, when we rescued them, Pond Flower and I really hit it off. She lives here most of the time."

"Except for when she comes to help you."

"Exactly."

Magic prickled on the air, but it wasn't dangerous. Just the signatures of the FireSouls who lived at the fortress.

"We're nearly there," I said.

A moment later, the tall, gray exterior wall appeared through the trees. It was built of massive blocks of stone. Though it was nearly impossible to get to the Arcadian forest because of its location at a waypoint, whoever had built the forest expected battle.

It'd been a while, though, and the tops of the ramparts were worn down. The space where two guards could stand was empty. Ivy had grown wild on big sections of the wall.

"Can we expect a warm welcome?" Roarke asked.

"I think so."

"I'd settle for anything that's not outright attack."

"Me too. But I think we'll be fine."

The dogs raced ahead, stopping at the massive wooden gate that blocked the entrance. They howled, their deep cries echoing through the forest.

A moment later, an irritated voice shouted, "Hang on, hang on!"

The gate began to creak open, and I could just make out the sound of a woman muttering, "Every hour of the day and night, these dogs set up a racket wanting to come in."

I grinned. This really had been the right place for the hellhounds.

Once the gate had creaked open, the dogs rushed inside. The woman looked up from them, her gaze widening at the sight of us. She reached for the sword at her waist, a quick move that looked instinctual, then lowered it.

"Del?" Corin asked. Her short blond hair and burnished red armor were just as I remembered.

"Corin. Good to see you." I walked forward, but she didn't step back to let us enter.

Her gaze darted to Roarke. "How did he get here? Who is he?"

"Roarke Fallon. Warden of the Underworld."

"Not one of us?" She didn't actually use the word *FireSoul*.

"No," he said. "Though I am sympathetic to your cause."

"And that might be?" she asked.

"You're FireSouls."

Quick as a flash, she drew her sword and pressed the tip to his throat. "I've heard of you. Stickler for the rules. And the rules don't like us."

"They don't." His head tilted slightly toward me. "But I like her. And I won't turn you in."

"He's legit," I said.

"You better be." Corin lowered her sword. "What are you doing here? How did you bring him?"

"I don't know."

"A non-FireSoul shouldn't be allowed through the portal. Unless you were touching him. I've heard that can work sometimes. Though we've never brought someone who wasn't our kind here. Not in my time."

"Just the hellhounds."

She smiled wryly. "They're an exception." She waved us in. "Come on in. Why are you here?"

"Do you have a Phantom dragon here?"

"A what?"

My heart sank. "If she were here, you wouldn't have missed her. She looks like a Phantom or a blue dragon."

"Dragons are dead. And there are no Phantoms here."

"I know. She's not a real dragon. She sent me here."

"I'm sorry, there are no Phantom dragons here. But maybe we can help you find out why she sent you here."

"Thanks." I followed her into the courtyard, wondering why Draka had sent me here.

Though run down, the place was magical. And I knew magic. There were ornate buildings and towers and turrets that twisted up into the sky. If four Rapunzels leaned out and waved at me, I wouldn't be surprised. Flower-covered vines climbed up the stone walls, curling over balconies. Tall grass grew in any area that wasn't covered by a path, and the fountains were dry.

It was built to hold hundreds of people. But only about a dozen FireSouls lived here, along with the hellhounds who'd disappeared somewhere.

"Why don't we go see Flora, the librarian?" Corin said. "She knows all kinds of things."

Maybe it would work, but I wasn't hopeful. For good measure, I called on my dragon sense, hoping it would give me an idea of *what* I was looking for here.

I got nothing. It was dead as a doornail.

Draka had led me here, but this was it.

"Seeing Flora sounds great, thanks." If anything, I just needed a place to sit down and think. The library had lots of chairs. And who knew? Maybe Flora would have some info.

Roarke and I followed Corin up the path. Though I heard voices a couple times, we saw no one else. It'd be easy to get lost in a place as large as this, though.

We entered a large stone building at the back of the fortress compound. Stepping into the main library room was like stepping into heaven. Massive wooden doors opened onto a large, oval-shaped room. Bookshelves soared to the ceiling three stories overhead. Balconies on each floor were accessed by seven spiral staircases. Circular, tower-shaped bookcases sat in the center of the room and extended two stories up. Tables and comfy chairs filled the rest of the space.

I'd only been here once before, but I hadn't wanted to leave. If I didn't have Draka to hunt for, Roarke would probably have to carry me out of this place.

We found the librarian in the middle of the room, just as we had last time. She sat at the largest table, which she'd piled high with books. She didn't look up as we approached, no doubt absorbed in her book.

I knew how that was.

"Flora," Corin said.

The pixie-looking woman didn't budge.

"Flora! Guests!" Corin shouted. Her voice echoed and I flinched. So did Roarke, who rarely showed any kind of reaction.

Flora looked up slowly. I wondered if she was hard of hearing or if she was just so stuck in her mind that Corin's voice didn't sound so loud. Flora blinked big green eyes at us. They were partially unfocused.

Yeah, stuck in that book big time. I wanted a peek.

Flora was fae as well as FireSoul, as far as I could tell, from her ears and the timeless quality about her. Though she looked young, I'd put money on her being nearly a hundred. Fae lived a damned long time.

"Flora? We have some questions for you."

"Again? You were here just yesterday." She nodded at me. "With her."

I glanced at Corin. I'd been here months ago. Corin shrugged slightly.

"All the same, if you have a moment, we'd really appreciate it," I said.

Flora nodded.

Corin met my gaze. "I'll leave you with her. When you're done, ask her to show you out."

"All right. Thank you."

Corin left, and I turned to Flora. "Thank you for answering my questions.

"It's fine." She sat back from the table. She'd been hunched over her book like a pretty gargoyle and now looked at least eight inches taller. "How can I help you?"

"I'm not sure, exactly," I said. "I was drawn here while looking for my friend Draka. She's a Phantom dragon."

Excitement flared in Flora's eyes, making her look fully alert for the first time. "Are you a Phantom?"

I stiffened. She shouldn't know that. No one should. But then, they wouldn't turn me in. Every person here, except for Roarke, was technically an illegal sort of supernatural. "How did you know that?"

"I didn't. But I was recently sent a message by a Phantom dragon."

"What kind of message?"

"One carried on blue smoke." Her gaze turned serious. "You must not seek your friend."

"Why the hell not?

"You must stay safe. You are the last of a dying breed from Snowdonia and hell. You cannot risk yourself."

Chills raced across my skin. Ever since Draka had disappeared, I'd been worried something bad had happened to her. "Risk myself? So she's in danger. If I seek her, I'll be in danger, too."

"You *must not* go after her."

"Where is she?"

"I do not know. But I was meant to pass this message." Her breathing sped up, like she was stressed.

I backed off the question, hoping to calm her, and went in another direction. "What do you mean, I'm the last of a dying breed from Snowdonia and hell? Is my family dead?"

My heart clenched in my chest as I awaited her response. I'd suspected this was the case, and my few memories of them weren't positive, but hearing it still made a greasy sickness rise in my stomach.

"Yes. They are dead."

I swallowed hard, my throat suddenly tightened painfully. Roarke's hand tightened on mine. I squeezed back, grateful that he was here.

"How could I be from Snowdonia and hell? That's not possible."

"Where else would a Phantom halfbreed's ancestral homeland be located, if not for Earth and hell?"

"Both?"

"Yes. But you're the last. You, and Draka. You must not risk it. With your role in the Triumvirate, you must not die."

"Dying isn't new to me. And I *won't* leave my friend if she needs me."

"There's nothing you can do for her," Flora said. "You will *not* go after Draka."

"*Will not?* You can't tell me what to do." Flora had confirmed my fears. Nothing would stop me. I'd felt Draka's love in my dreams. She would do the same for me.

Flora's gaze turned sad. "You'll try to go after her."

"Tell me anything you can to help me," I begged. "Increase my chances."

She shook her head. "No. I know nothing. And you will not go."

I pushed away from the table, rising. Roarke followed.

"Thank you for the help, Flora." I turned to leave.

"You will not go." The power in her voice sent a shiver of stark fear across my skin. I'd never heard such power in a being's voice. Not even in Roarke's.

Was it some strange fae magic?

I let my ice power rise inside of me. I wouldn't kill her. No way I could do that. But if I had to defend myself...defend Draka....

I spun around just in time to see Flora's eyes flare wide and flash green as acid. She flung out her hands and screamed, "You will not go!"

The air around me turned gelatinous. It was clear enough to see Flora, whose hair now waved in an invisible wind of her power, but it was thick around my limbs, binding them tight to my sides.

Frantic, I glanced at Roarke out of the corners of my eyes as I struggled to break free.

He was bound too! The veins in his neck bulged with strain as he fought to free himself. But it didn't work.

I could feel Flora's power on the air, like electricity crackling against my skin. Through the air that bound us, she looked wild.

Her mousey exterior and piles of books had hidden a fae of the most incredible power.

It was always the bookish ones you had to be worried about. They knew shit. And Flora knew some powerful magic. No matter how much I strained, I couldn't break free.

She held out her hands toward us, her gaze still an acid green. Magic flowed from her palms, drifting toward us. I'd never seen magic behave quite like that before. Eerie.

Sweat broke out on my skin.

Roarke and I slowly drifted backwards until our backs were pressed against the wall.

"You must stay there." Flora's voice was still as deep and powerful as it had been, though softer. "The magic will not harm you. I will release you soon, when it is safe. I promised."

I tried to open my mouth to demand answers. *When it is safe!? Promised to who?* But my jaw was solidly shut, bound by magic.

Flora's gaze turned sad, and the acid green faded to the normal grassy shade. When she spoke, her voice was back to normal. Wispy and distant. She was barely seeing us now; she was so far back into her usual distant land.

"It is truly a shame, to lose all the Phantom dragons with the one." Her gaze flicked up to me. "But we need you. The Triumvirate needs you. The world needs you."

What the heck was I supposed to do with that? Frustration was a balloon growing in my chest.

"She was clear. And this must be done." Flora turned and walked back to her desk, then sat and pulled a book over.

Stupefied, I stared at her. Even if I had been able to move or talk, I probably wouldn't have been able to.

She was just going to sit there, reading like normal? And leave us here in this weird prison?

It was insane.

There was no way she could get away with it. Someone would come in here eventually and find us.

As if I'd called her, Corin stepped through the library door a moment later. Like a true warrior, she surveyed the room the way I was sure she did anytime she entered. It was habit, ingrained after years of being hunted.

"Did they leave?" she asked Flora.

Flora didn't look up.

"Flora!"

Flora startled, jerking her hazy gaze up to meet Corin's. "Leave?"

"Yes, Del and her friend Roarke."

Inside, I screamed like a banshee, trying to get Corin's attention. It didn't work.

"Oh, yes." Flora shook her head as if to clear it. If she were acting, I totally bought it. She could get a dozen Oscars for this performance. "I helped them with a question about their friend and walked them out."

No! Frustration beat at my chest with fists of iron.

"They didn't need anything else?"

"No."

"Perfect." Corin smiled. "See you later, Flora."

When Corin turned to leave, I caught sight of her expression. My hope shriveled to dust.

She trusted Flora. Implicitly. And didn't question a single thing she'd just heard.

Oh, fates. We are in trouble.

CHAPTER FOUR

Roarke and I stood for hours, just watching Flora read. The lights had dimmed, and I felt like a toy forgotten on the shelf. Early on, I'd tried adopting my Phantom form to see if I could drift out of this prison. I'd failed. So my mind spun like a hamster in a wheel while the rest of me did nothing but float.

The spell that trapped us was completely comfortable—no aches or pains or hunger, even though I'd digested my muffin hours ago. But that was worse. It meant that this magic was meant to keep us in stasis for however long Flora needed.

As relaxed and comfortable as my body was, my mind was a carnival of fear, worry, and frustration. Escape plans disappeared as quickly as they formed. There was no way out of this.

Occasionally, I managed to steal a glance at Roarke out of the corner of my eye. My eyeballs seemed to be the only things I could move—I couldn't even blink my eyelids. He looked alternately frustrated and utterly baffled. Like he'd never experienced anything with this much power over him.

Which made sense. Up until now, he was the most powerful being I'd ever met besides Cass and Aidan.

But Flora....

No one had seen Flora coming. People always underestimated the bookworms. I should have known better, being a bookworm myself.

Idiot.

Finally, Flora yawned, stretching her arms over her head.

Was it already night?

She pushed away from the table and rose, not sparing us a glance as she left.

Oh, fates, I hoped she remembered she'd put us here. I had no idea how long she meant to keep us here, but if she forgot about us...

I wanted to scream.

No. Think, think, *think*.

There had to be a way out. My Phantom power had failed. Ice could do nothing here. I could try to use the Ubilaz demon's power to attract other demons. Until now, I had just repressed it so that other demons didn't find me. But maybe if a bunch of them attacked, it would cause enough commotion that we might get out somehow.

Immediately, I felt like a jerk.

Not only was that a bad idea—I'd probably just get killed while standing here frozen like a popsicle—but I'd throw my FireSoul friends under the bus. Because the

League of FireSouls were my friends. They'd helped us in the past when we'd needed them.

Granted, Flora was being difficult right now, but she had her reasons.

I couldn't bring demons here.

All afternoon, I'd been trying to call Pond Flower to me. It hadn't worked, but I tried again anyway. I had no idea if the hellhound could hear me, but *please, fates,* let me get lucky.

We may have waited hours or minutes, I couldn't tell, but finally—*finally*—I heard the click of hellhound toenails on the shining wooden floors. Hope flared in my chest as Pond Flower padded into view.

Her gaze found me immediately. Could she see me, even though Corin hadn't been able to?

Her black nose twitched and she approached. About six inches before her nose would have touched my waist, it thudded into an invisible barrier. Confusion entered her warm eyes, and she sniffed harder.

Then she turned and left the room.

I screamed like I'd never screamed before. Not a sound escaped my lips, but I heard every decibel in my head like I was at a freaking Justin Bieber concert and the Beebs had refused to show. There was *rage,* and it was *loud.*

If I could have kicked things, I would have.

Normally, inaction killed me. Jumping before I looked was a flaw of mine. But this wasn't just inaction. This was torture.

I had no idea how long I threw my silent but debilitating mental hissy fit, but when Pond Flower showed up with twelve of her closest friends trailing behind, my mind went blank with excitement.

It revved back into gear pretty quickly, but the best it could manage was a weak, *What the hell?*

The dogs gathered around me and Roarke, noses twitching. I couldn't feel them, but I almost thought I could smell the brimstone scent of their magic. They were all different colors—black and brown and cream—but their eyes all flared with red fire as their magic swelled. Black flames grew up from their fur, flickering eerily in the dim light of the library.

There was no heat, just magic. It grew stronger and stronger, the scent of brimstone so fierce that I almost gagged.

Would the other FireSouls sense it?

Fates, I hoped not. At least not until the hellhounds finished whatever it was they were doing.

Please let it be releasing us.

The slightest breeze brushed my cheek, the first thing I'd felt in hours. My heart sped up. They were trying to spring us!

Hellhounds had powerful, obscure magic. This might actually work. My hand itched to knock on my head, but it wouldn't budge no matter how hard I tried. So I settled for just begging fate.

A moment later, I could blink my eyes. Then move my jaw.

"You there?" I asked Roarke, trying to turn my head. It took a moment for that to work out, but it did.

Finally, Roarke said, "Yes."

"What the hell is going on?" The feminine voice made my stomach drop. We were only half free!

I whipped my gaze toward the voice and saw the familiar tall, blond warrior. Her short hair was sleep-mussed, and her pajama pants had cats on them.

"Corin! Thank fates," I said.

The hellhounds kept up their magical black flame, burning away the barrier Flora had created.

"What happened to you?" Corin demanded.

"Flora put us here for some reason. She said she'd promised someone." Draka?

Corin shook her head, her gaze knowing. "She may have. Flora's weird, but she's old and powerful. Other old, powerful beings sometimes come to her for help."

That fit Draka perfectly.

"Be that as it may, we're getting out of here," Roarke said.

I could finally move my arms, so I hiked my thumb toward him. "I'm with him."

Corin nodded. "Fine. I'm going to go wait outside, make sure Flora doesn't come back. But once these hellhounds free you, run for it. We may be able to hold Flora off, but she's strong."

"Thank you."

"Not a problem." She headed for the door.

"Come on, guys, hurry." I petted Pond Flower's head where it hovered near my hip. Their black flame magic, which didn't burn my skin, had almost disintegrated the spell all the way down to our calves. *Just a little farther.*

"Flora underestimated the hellhounds," Roarke said. "And your bond with them. These dogs normally don't help anyone."

"They're good dogs." Pond Flower's head was warm under my hand.

"You're special."

A moment later, the last of the charm broke free of my legs. I stumbled, but the dogs caught me by crowding in front of me.

"Let's move." I met Pond Flower's fiery red gaze. "Can you lead the way? Fast?"

Understanding filled her eyes and she turned, racing from the library. Her friends sprinted off behind her, and Roarke and I followed.

We made it through the hall and past Corin, then out onto the main courtyard before we heard the bellow.

"Stop!" Flora's power-filled voice was deep as the oceans.

I sprinted harder, following the hellhounds across the courtyard to the main gate. Flora's magic welled in the air. My legs began to slow.

That damned trapping spell!

"Pond Flower!" I called.

She whirled, powerful haunches sending her back my way. She and her fellows sprinted behind us, facing Flora. Their brimstone smell of magic surged. I risked a glance behind me to see the hellhounds forming a line between us and Flora, who stood in the middle of the courtyard in black sweatpants with her hair all spiked up from sleep. Black flames rose up from the hellhounds' fur—a barrier.

Flora's looks were deceptive—you wouldn't think she was a massively powerful supernatural being. But the hellhounds' protective barrier was too much for her.

The magic that slowed my legs faded. I sprinted harder, Roarke at my side. We raced through the gate and through the forest, down the trail, leaping over rocks and boulders to reach the portal.

At some point, Pond Flower joined us, sprinting alongside, her tongue lolling in the wind. Joy surged through me.

As much as today had possessed some sucky moments, being rescued by a hellhound was pretty badass.

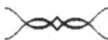

"Holy fates, that was nuts." I slumped in Roarke's car as he zoomed away from the forest.

"We're just lucky you're friends with that dog."

"Seriously." Pond Flower had escorted us all the way back to the car, racing alongside. Either her magic had kept the redwood forest's enchantments away, or they only worked when you were approaching the portal.

Either way, I was grateful.

My mind raced. There was so much to process.

"Draka doesn't want us to come after her," I said. "Did she want us trapped like that?"

Roarke shrugged one big shoulder. "Couldn't say."

"I'm going after her. She's in danger."

"I did get that impression."

A hundred scenarios flashed in my head. What was wrong with her? Where *was* she? And what about my family? My heart clenched in my chest, a visceral pain.

When Roarke took the turn for his place instead of the road leading back into Magic's Bend, I glanced at him. "We're headed to your place?"

"I can take you home if you prefer," he said.

"No." I didn't want to be in my house right now. My home was so normal. So much like my old life. But that life was gone. It'd ended weeks ago when I'd been killed in battle and woken in hell.

I was back from the dead. A Phantom.

An orphan.

Was I too old to be an orphan? Did it matter?

"Are you all right?" Roarke asked as he pulled the car to a stop in the drive. The massive trees around his house stood silent sentry.

"Yeah. Fine." I rubbed a hand over my face. "I just don't know quite how to feel about all this. About my parents. Them being dead. I'm sad, but also not."

"It can't be easy."

"No, I suppose not." I glanced at the house, suddenly longing to start fresh. To wash away everything that had happened and clear my mind. I needed to focus on what I could *do*, not what I had lost. Or maybe never had. "I'm going to shower, okay?"

"Sure. I'll get us something to eat."

I smiled at him gratefully. "You're a hero."

If I was honest with myself, I loved that he always had my back in a fight. After my life with my *deirfiúr*, that was how I qualified love. But what I *really, really* loved was that this badass, scary Warden of the Underworld had a thing for getting me food.

I wasn't a big eater, not like Cass or Nix for whom it was a bit of a hobby, but the fact that he took care of me was nice. *Really* nice.

The air was chilly as I climbed out of the car and hurried into the house, but Roarke's place was as welcoming as ever. The warm wood glowed, and the rustic chic furnishings made me feel welcome.

I made quick work of my shower, trying not to think of my dead parents, then snuck out onto the balcony to call Cass and Nix. I didn't have anything to hide from Roarke, but I just wanted to talk to them alone.

The sun was setting as I leaned against the railing and stared down at the glittering river that tumbled over boulders. I pressed my fingertip to my comms charm to ignite its magic. "Cass? Nix?"

"Where are you?" Cass asked.

"Yeah, spill," Nix said. "Do you need help?"

I felt better just hearing their voices. I may have lost my parents, probably long before they were even dead, given my memories, but I had family. I had them. I had Draka.

"I don't know," I said. It took a while, but I told them everything I'd learned.

"I'm so sorry," Cass said when I told her about my parents. "That sucks."

"Thanks." I didn't want to dwell on it. "I'm going to go after Draka, though. I have to."

"Do you even know where to go?" Nix asked.

Neither Nix nor Cass bothered to tell me it was too dangerous—that Draka didn't want me to come for her. It wasn't our way.

"My only clue is Snowdonia, where I'm supposedly from." The mountain range in Wales wasn't far from the quarry cave where the four Phantom dragons had lived, so it made sense. "I'm going to start there.

"Smart," Cass said. "We'll come to help."

"You don't have to."

"Ha! Dream on," Cass said. "Actually, do that while getting a good night's sleep. Then we'll be at Roarke's place early tomorrow, and we'll go to Wales."

I was tired enough that I agreed. Though I wanted to set off now, I was still feeling pretty beat up after our journey through the redwood forest. A few hours sleep would make me better able to rescue Draka.

"Thanks, guys."

"Duh, anytime," Nix said.

I smiled.

After finishing up with Nix and Cass, I left the porch. My cheeks were icy from the cold, but the rest of me was toasty in my polar bear fleece PJs. A couple days ago, after our visit to the Underworld to deal with my out-of-control Ubilaz demon powers, I'd given Roarke a small duffel bag of my clothes to take to his place.

We were nowhere near official as a couple or whatever, but the duffel bag full of clothes meant something. It hadn't seemed like a big deal until now, but pulling my own clothes out of a drawer in his house made this feel serious.

And serious made me nervous.

The Allman Brothers were playing on the speakers when I made my way down the wide wooden staircase to the first floor.

The spacious living room was empty, but Roarke had started a fire in the big fireplace and a box of red wine sat on the coffee table.

He must've had good ears because as soon as I hit the living room, he shouted from the kitchen, "You can have a seat out there if you want. I'll bring it in."

"Thanks!" I curled up on the plush couch and stared into the flames, letting the comfort wash over me.

A moment later, he walked out carrying two big bowls. "Spaghetti." He handed me one, and I took it gratefully.

"Looks like fancy spaghetti," I said. The sauce was covered in freshly grated parmesan and smelled divine.

"Not as fancy as it could be." He sat next to me, and I couldn't help but be aware of the sheer size of him.

"You really like to cook, huh?" I took a bite and hummed in appreciation. "That really is a bit too perfect. You're a dude. Shouldn't you be surviving off take-out and hot dogs?"

He laughed. "Stereotype much? But I like cooking. It makes me feel more normal."

He'd called it a hobby once, but now there was a slight wistfulness in his voice. It sounded like more than a hobby. "Normal?"

He nodded. The firelight warmed his features, making him even more handsome. "Don't get me wrong. I like being Warden of the Underworld. I don't want a nine-to-five. But I spend most of my time in hell dealing with demons and the worst of the worst. That can give a guy a skewed perspective. It's good to try to have a normal life outside of that. With cooking and a house that doesn't smell like brimstone."

I sniffed the air, getting a nice hint of the cedar wood scent of his house and the rich aroma of tomatoes. "Smells pretty good in here to me. Not a trace of brimstone."

But it made sense, what he was saying. Given his size and strength, he looked more like a Warden of the Underworld Break the Demons in Half type than a *Top-Chef* type, but I liked the contrast.

"I try."

I'd polished off the last of my spaghetti and was reaching for my mug of wine when he spoke again.

"What is the Triumvirate? Flora mentioned it."

My grip tightened on the mug. "A prophecy. About me, Cass, and Nix. You know how you said I was special?"

He nodded and I took a sip of wine before continuing. "Well, I think that may be why. Triumvirate means Three of Power. Cass represents magic, Nix is life, and I'm death. We were each prophesied to accomplish a great task. We think that Cass accomplished hers when she killed the Monster. But me…"

"You haven't accomplished yours yet."

"Exactly. Though I'm thinking that maybe this Guardian and Demise thing that Draka told me about could be part of it." Just the thought made my head spin. I didn't want to be something called the Demise. That had *bad* written all over it.

I glanced up at Roarke, who'd set his bowl on the table and now lounged on the couch, looking like some massive were-demon slash superhot football player hybrid. The firelight flickered on his dark hair, and his sweater clung to the curves of his muscles.

My mind went straight to the gutter, wondering what he'd feel like beneath that shirt. And what would he look like? I'd only ever gotten a good look at him in his were-demon form. And while that held a certain scary, animal appeal, I had a feeling I'd prefer the human Roarke.

I licked my lips, my gaze riveted to his face. He glanced from the fire toward me and suddenly, I didn't want to just look.

I wanted to touch. Not just because I didn't want to think about my confusing life for a while, but because I wanted him.

I climbed over a few feet and knelt at his side, gripping his shirt and yanking him toward me a bit.

His brows rose, but the surprise was quickly replaced by heat. His dark eyes turned pitch black and roved over my face.

What was going on inside his head?

"It's not that I don't want to talk about that stuff," I murmured. "It's just that I don't know anything else. And I can think of a lot better ways to spend our time."

"Can you?"

The rough timbre of his voice made me shiver. "Yeah."

"Why don't you tell me about it?" His hand rested on my hip, burning me through my clothes.

Tell him? I was more of a *do* kind of girl. Telling sounded scary. But from the heat in his gaze, it looked like he wanted to hear me say it.

And from the warmth that grew inside me, I wanted to tell him. It was scary, but whatever. Life was scary.

"I want to touch you. Kiss you." It was tame, but from the way his hand tightened on my hip, he liked it. Every muscle in his body was tense and his gaze ravenous.

"Go ahead." His voice was rough.

My breath caught in my throat. I didn't hesitate, just leaned in and pressed my lips to his. He groaned low in his throat, almost a growl, then yanked me onto him.

My heart thundered in my ears as I wrapped my arms around his neck and straddled him. He was hot and hard beneath me, a million miles of muscles.

His big hand cupped the back of my head as his lips plundered my own. My head spun, and my heart raced as I absorbed the taste and feel of him.

Roarke was the best kisser in the world. Strong and sure and talented.

I ran my hands over his big shoulders and down his arms, debating reaching between us and yanking off my shirt.

I gasped. "We need to stop."

I wasn't ready for that yet. And I barely knew him, for fate's sake. I wasn't used to moving this fast, but he was making me lose my mind. Kissing was one thing. Tearing off my clothes was another.

He stilled abruptly, drawing his head back. "Are you okay?"

"Fine." I smiled. "Just don't want to move too fast."

The corner of his mouth tugged up in a small smile. "No problem. We could both use a good night's sleep anyway."

I nodded, climbing off him and mourning the loss of his heat. My every muscle and nerve still vibrated with want, and Roarke was tense as a wire pulled taught. I was about a half second away from saying, 'Screw it,' and jumping on him. And screwing something else.

Roarke stood, towering over me, and reached for my hand. I let his fingers close around mine, then followed him up the stairs.

He was about to leave me at the bedroom that I'd borrowed last time when I tugged at him.

"I'd rather sleep with you," I said.

He turned to face me, surprise on his face.

"Sleep. Just sleep," I said.

He grinned. "That works for me. I might not be able to sleep much next to you, but I'm willing to try."

"Good."

CHAPTER FIVE

Cold blasted me as soon as the ether spit us out in Wales. The wind whipped my hair as I stumbled back from Cass and looked around.

The five of us—me, Cass, Nix, Roarke, and Aidan—stood on top of a bleak mountaintop. It wasn't a quarry like the one Roarke and I had visited before, but rather an untouched, snow-covered peak. More mountains stretched into the distance in all directions.

Cass had transported us all here. They'd arrived early that morning, making me hop out of bed before they caught me and peppered me with questions. Sleeping next to Roarke had been lovely, but I wasn't up for a discussion about it.

After a hasty breakfast, we'd headed out immediately. Flora's clue about Snowdonia was all I had to go on, so we'd chosen the highest peak on the map. From here, we'd use our dragon senses to try to find my home. Proximity often helped, so hopefully we were close enough.

"This is as close as I can get us," Cass said. "What do you think?"

I looked around, not recognizing anything. My dragon sense tugged. "We're still fairly far away. I can sort of tell where it might be, but it's fuzzy. Magic must be protecting the location."

"Makes sense," Aidan said. "It'd be poor security to allow someone to transport right to your door."

"Like Hogwarts," Nix added. She was a *Harry Potter* buff—a member of House Ravenclaw according to the online quizzes she loved. "You aren't allowed to apparate into Hogwarts."

"Basically like that," Aidan said.

"Then we should be ready for more security," Roarke said. "Where to next?"

I reached for my magic, letting it flow through me. Snowflakes gathered on my eyelashes as I let my desire to find my ancestral homeland fill my chest.

The slightest tug pulled me north, so I raised a hand and pointed. "That way."

I shared a glance with Roarke, who stood out starkly in black snow gear, then huddled into my own down jacket and set off. We hiked through the snow in a small group. I could just pick up the slight buzz of everyone's magical signatures. We were all on high alert, and our magic was roaring.

I had no idea what to expect, but whatever it was, it'd be well protected. Though this was a remote place for supernaturals to live, it wasn't remote enough. If Flora was right and this was where I was from, my ancestors wouldn't have wanted humans showing up on their doorstep and would have been prepared with protective magic.

"So you've got no idea what this place will look like?" Cass asked.

"No. I remember nothing." I'd had nightmares all night, imagining what it would be like. "The best I've got is that there is a tower somewhere."

Like in the dreams I'd had before, about being a young girl locked in the tower, practicing my sword play. I'd seen mountains through the windows. Probably these mountains.

I led us up a steep slope. The snow grew thicker the farther we climbed. My feet sank into the snow, deeper and deeper with each step. Soon, it was up to our ankles. Then to our calves.

I'd worn decent boots with my snow gear—I wasn't about to head to a place called Snowdonia in the winter without something warm—but the cold stuff was starting to sneak in at the hem of my pants, an icy touch that made me shudder.

"Hang on, guys." Nix stopped abruptly, and her magic swelled, the faint scent of flowers fresh against the chill air.

A moment later, a pile of snowshoes appeared at her feet.

"Thanks!" I bent and picked up a pair, strapping them to my feet.

Everyone else did the same. I took a few tentative steps. It was weird, but better than sinking in the snow.

"These are excellent, thank you," Roarke said.

Cass and Aidan mirrored his sentiments, and we took off again, going single file up a ridge of mountain. In the distance, the peaks rolled on. Snow began to fall, sticking to my eyelashes and turning my nose into an icicle.

"Do you hear that?" Roarke asked from ahead of me.

I shoved my hat off my ears so I could hear better. A dull roaring sound echoed over the snow. "Yeah, weird."

"Sounds like water," Aidan said.

"Agreed." Roarke picked up the pace, and I hurried behind, sweating more with every step. It might've been freezing cold, but this hike was heating me up.

We crested a ridge, and I stopped dead in my tracks, my jaw dropping low. The ridge we'd climbed wasn't actually at the highest point. No—ahead of us stood two tall gray cliffs. Between them poured a massive waterfall into a beautiful blue pool.

"How the hell is it not frozen solid?" Nix demanded.

"Not cold enough?" Cass asked.

"Oh, it's plenty cold enough," Nix said. "And where is it coming from? There shouldn't be a river big enough in this part of Wales to feed that thing. Especially not here."

"I don't think we're in Kansas anymore." I couldn't take my gaze away from the waterfall. It poured so fast and so hard that it was pure white as it pounded into the pool below. The pool itself glittered the deep, bright turquoise of a glacier lake. I'd never seen such a beautiful color in my life. It made my eyes hurt to look at it. The bank was white snow and the whole scene postcard perfect.

"No, you're right. This is strange," Roarke said. "Wales has some pretty impressive mountains, and they can get snowy, but this is year-round, thousand-year-old, Everest-type snow. That's off. This is magic."

The dangerous kind.

Aidan stepped forward, his arms crossed over his chest as he stared up. "We can't climb those cliffs."

"We can try flying over them." Roarke took off his snowshoes.

Aidan nodded. "It may be the only way."

I stepped back as the tornado of gray mist began to swirl around Roarke. Golden light glowed from Aidan as his magic took hold. It was pretty spectacular to watch them both shift at the same time, especially against the backdrop of pure white snow.

Their magic swelled on the air, competing scents of forest and sandalwood. A moment later, the dark demon-angel and the griffin stood before us.

As usual, the magic had removed Roarke's jacket and shirt so his wings wouldn't destroy them, but he wore the same pants and boots. His dark wings were stark against the snow. The griffin was protected by his golden fur and feathers. Honestly, Aidan looked warmer in that form.

Roarke lifted his wings, then brought them down in a powerful motion.

His feet didn't leave the ground. He frowned.

Beside him, Aidan crouched low, ready to push off into the air and take flight with his massive golden wings.

He pushed off like I expected, but he went nowhere. His feet were stuck like glue.

"Magic." Roarke's gravelly voice was thick with annoyance. "No flying. Like at the quarry."

Shit. The magic wanted to force us to go a certain way.

Golden light enveloped the griffin. A moment later, Aidan stood in its place and said, "Security measure."

"Which way are we supposed to go, then?" I studied the scene ahead. The two cliff faces were unclimbable. Not only were they sheer gray rock, but further examination revealed that they were covered by a thick sheet of shiny ice. On the far side of each cliff was nothing. Just air. No way around.

"I think we have to go under the waterfall," Nix said.

My dragon sense tugged that way. The waterfall, though powerful, didn't look thick. There was space behind it. Occasionally, I thought I could make out the shadow of something.

There was no denying it. That was where we needed to be. So we were going to have to jump into that icy water and swim under the waterfall.

"I think you're right," I said.

Aidan frowned. "Going to be cold."

"And there could be enchantments," Cass said. "Actually, I'd bank on it."

"Me too." Dread curled in the pit of my stomach. I'd almost drowned back at the lake when I'd had to fight the lake monster. My throat burned at the memory of hacking up water.

"It's not a thick waterfall, though," Nix said. "It's powerful, but there's not far we have to swim underwater."

I hoped she was right. I started toward the edge of the pond, treading carefully on the snow. The pool was deep, the middle a pure, dark blue that could only come from some serious water depth. Up close, the roar of the water was deafening.

"I do not like the look of that." I stepped forward, but pulled up short before my foot could hit the ground.

The magic felt a bit funny. Prickly—but so faint.

I reached out a hand, hitting an invisible wall. Then I grinned.

"Why the smile?" Cass asked. "Because this looks pretty dire."

"There's an invisible protective barrier here." I laid my palm flat against the barrier, probably looking like a mime. "The past few times, I've just walked into these and slammed my face. But this time! This time I learned. Felt it right before I hit it."

"Practice makes perfect," Nix said.

Aidan stepped up and ran his hands over the barrier that protected the pool. "This may be why it doesn't freeze in the cold. But we still have to get through it."

"I can break it," Roarke said.

"If the barrier is broken, will the cold freeze the water and trap us underneath?" I asked.

"Not if we're fast," Cass said.

"Then we'd better be fast," Aidan said.

"We'll be okay," Nix said.

"Don't jinx us." I knocked on my head. "I think we need a plan."

"Agreed," Cass said. "Aidan and I will shift into polar bears. That should help."

I swung my head toward her. "Polar bears? Well, I guess they don't fly, so it should work."

"And polar bears are great swimmers," Cass added. "If any of us falters, the bears can help. Also, I've always wanted to be a polar bear. And they're printed on your lucky PJs, so it's got to bring us luck."

I hoped she was right. But I was feeling pretty lucky to have all of them around right now. Every one of them had skills we needed. As the Origin, a descendent of the first ever shifter, Aidan could change into any type of animal he wanted. Cass was a Mirror Mage, and as such, she could mimic his magic.

"Okay." I turned back to the pool. "So you guys shift, Roarke will break the barrier, then we'll swim for it."

"And remember," Cass said. "If you use up half your air supply and you don't see the end, turn back around. Make it back out alive."

A key rule of treasure hunting. Stay alive.

Everyone nodded.

Magic surged as Aidan and Cass shifted. A moment later, two massive white bears stood beside me. Aidan was bigger, with silky white fur and jet black eyes, but I wouldn't have wanted to run into Cass in the wild, either.

They were terrifying, but also damned cute.

"I really just want to cuddle up with you guys." I took off my snowshoes, then turned to Roarke, who was still in demon form. He was stronger this way. "Ready?"

"As ever." He approached the barrier, swung back his fist, then sent it hurtling toward the barrier.

His fist stopped in midair, colliding with the barrier with a deafening crash and sending crackling white lines streaking across the air like broken glass.

He stepped forward, through the barrier and right up to the very edge of the pond, then turned back to me. "Go time."

I nodded and shared an anxious glance with Nix. We nodded at each other. On the far side, the bears nodded, too. Roarke turned to the water. I sucked in a deep breath and ran for the water, side by side with my friends, and dived in.

Tiny icicles pierced me all over. It was even colder than Lake Laberge. I kicked as hard as I could, fighting through the water. I hadn't dove deep, but every foot of this water felt like a mile.

When my head broke the surface, I didn't stop. Just kept kicking toward the waterfall. The pressure of the water pounding down vibrated through my chest. When we neared it, I dove deep, opening my eyes to make sure I was going in the right direction.

The water glittered clear and blue. As soon as I kicked under the fall of water, I tumbled end over end, caught in the force of the flow. I thrashed and kicked. Out of the corner of my eye, I could see Roarke and Nix in the same position.

My lungs burned as I struggled. The water was stronger than it should've been.

Enchantment.

Desperate, I fought to get free of the pull, but it forced me deeper. I no longer felt the cold tearing at my skin. Panic heated my blood and made me fight, kicking and clawing at the water.

But I went nowhere.

A moment later, something hard shoved me from behind, forcing me free of the enchantment. Suddenly, my strokes carried me through the water. I kicked as hard as I could, using the last of my strength to reach the glowing surface above.

Almost there!

My lungs burned, desperate for the air that was so close. With a powerful kick, I reached the surface.

And crashed into a sheet of ice.

An involuntary scream escaped my throat, costing me precious air.

Panicked, I beat at the ice above my head, but it didn't break. It was so damned thick.

I spun in the water, my hair floating around my head and making it hard to see. Where were my friends?

Nix was swimming toward me, her eyes wide and her skin pale. A polar bear behind her pushed Roarke free of the water trap, then swam for us.

Frantically, I pointed at the ice above my head. The bear looked at it, then swam for it with powerful legs. It crashed into the ice, clearly hoping to break it.

But the ice was too thick. The bear slammed into it again, but the ice held.

Black started to creep in at the edges of my vision.

No!

We needed air!

The other polar bear swam up to join us, its dark gaze on the ice. It pressed its paws against the ice. They glowed red.

Fire! Cass was using her gift of fire to melt the ice!

I strained to stay calm and conserve the last of my air, but my lungs were burning. Cass's fire was so slow. She wasn't even halfway through the sheet of ice above when she withdrew her paws. I wanted to scream, but didn't dare lose the air.

Cass the bear swam down a bit, then pushed up through the water and crashed into the thinned sheet of ice. It exploded upward, rocking me back.

Through blurry vision, I saw the bear drop back into the water and swim down beneath me. Beside me, the other bear caught Nix. They pushed us up through the water until I could catch hold of the edge of the ice.

I sucked in delicious air as soon as my head broke the surface. My muscles felt like noodles as I tried to pull myself out. Mostly, the bear shoved me out like cargo. Nix came through the hole after me.

A moment later, Roarke climbed through under his own power, though he was much slower than normal. Even his demon form didn't give him enough strength to handle this. Then two giant, sopping wet polar bears climbed up.

Numb, I flopped back on the ice and stared at the sharp blue sky, sucking air into my aching lungs. We all sprawled out on the ice, exhausted.

Unfortunately, the numbness disappeared quickly and was followed by the most aching cold. I shook with it.

Magic swirled on the air with Cass's signature. And Aidan's. A moment later, Cass stood over me. Because she'd shifted, her clothes were still dry. It'd taken her a while to learn to keep her clothes when she changed. I'd bet she was glad for the practice now.

"Come on, dude." She bent and hauled me up.

I slumped against her, legs as wobbly as jello. Upright, I was finally able to check out our surroundings.

They were almost identical to where we'd just been.

Damn it. I'd hoped we'd be on the front doorstep.

"We have to get you warmed up," Aidan said. He had his arm wrapped around Nix's waist. "You're hypothermic and about halfway dead."

"Ha!" I was pretty sure I'd been halfway dead for a while now. Ever since I'd woken in hell.

Roarke made it to his feet himself, probably a product of his enhanced demon strength, but he was a much paler gray than usual.

As a raggedy group, we stumbled over to the snow piled up on the other side of the pool.

"Do you think the pool on this side was supposed to be frozen?" My teeth chattered as I talked.

"I don't know." Cass pointed to a shallow cave in the rock. "We're headed there."

By the time we made it to the cave, I was ready to collapse. Cass sat me in the snow, then turned and built a bonfire with her magic. I huddled close for warmth, my teeth chattering so hard I thought they would break. The wind was bitter here, cutting through my wet clothes like knives.

Roarke plopped down beside me, wrapping a strong arm around my shoulders. Warmth flowed through me immediately, and I sighed as I sank into him. It wasn't enough to warm me fully, but it felt *amazing*.

"I've got this." Nix's voice was slurred from exhaustion and cold, but her magic rose strong on the air.

Two large tents popped out of nowhere, conjured with her gift, then piles of snowsuits and a few thermoses.

"Y-you're a-amazing," I stuttered.

Aidan and Cass bent for the thermoses as the rest of us scrambled to our feet and collected fresh clothes, then we headed into the tents where we could change without snow climbing into our new clothes. And in this bitter wind, I didn't want to get buck naked. Modesty had flown the coop right around the time I almost drowned under the ice.

Roarke followed me into the larger tent, shifting back to human form as soon as we made it inside. His shirt returned with his human form, so it was dry, but his pants were still soaking wet.

Ah, the limits of magic.

I tried to chuckle to myself, but my throat appeared to be frozen shut. This would have been a perfect time to check out Roarke getting dressed, but I didn't want to be a creeper.

And frankly, I was too cold to do anything but shiver as I struggled out of my wet clothes and into the new ones, grateful that Nix knew my size and had a knack for conjuring knitwear and ski apparel.

When I was finally dressed, I was lying on my back and panting, so exhausted from the struggle that I thought I might never move again.

Roarke sat by my side and hauled me up against him. I sank into his warmth again.

"Good thing your friends are here," he said.

"Yeah." Finally, my teeth didn't chatter when I spoke.

"Let's go see how everyone is doing."

I didn't want to get up and leave the tent, but there was a fire out there. And my friends. Who deserved a solid thank you. I nodded and followed him out of the tent.

Aidan and Cass sat around the fire, warming their hands. Nix was climbing out of her tent at the same time we were.

"Feeling better?" Cass asked.

"Yeah. Thanks for saving us. You were right about the polar bears." I turned to Nix. "And thanks for the clothes."

"Not a problem." She rubbed her arms for warmth as she hurried to the fire.

We all huddled around the fire, soaking in the warmth and recovering our strength. The hot chocolate that Nix had conjured tasted amazing, and I passed it to Roarke. He took it with a nod of thanks and grinned.

"So, your house is pretty well protected," Nix said.

"Yeah." I didn't even want to know what the place looked like. We weren't at the driveway yet, and we'd almost died.

"Do you think we're close?" Roarke asked.

"I hope so."

We spent nearly an hour huddled around the fire, recovering from the ordeal. Most of my jobs—whether it was demon hunting or treasure hunting—were strenuous. But this was new territory.

"Ready to move on?" I asked.

"Yeah." Nix sighed and stood. She glanced at the tents. "We'll have to come back for these. I hate to litter."

"Sure." While Nix could conjure things, she couldn't make them disappear. Not yet, anyway.

I took a moment to call on my dragon sense and get my bearings. It picked up the trail easily, tugging me toward it. I pointed west. "That way."

We set off, tromping across the snow. On this side of the waterfall, at least the white stuff was harder packed and we didn't need the snow shoes.

As we walked, a mist rolled across the mountains. It was thick and white, an eerie accompaniment to the ever-whitening world we hiked through. In the course of seconds, it obscured everything around me.

The entire world was white.

"Guys?" I called. "We need to stick close together. This mist is thick."

There was nothing but silence. Goosebumps popped up on my skin. This was scarier than everything we'd just been through. I *knew* what lurked on this mountain.

My heart thudded as I spun in a circle, searching. "Cass, Nix? Roarke?"

Nothing. Not a sound—not even the wind. Just biting cold and nothingness. "Guys!"

No answer.

Oh, shit.

CHAPTER SIX

Something was wrong. I called on my dragon sense, feeding it my desire to find my friends. But no matter how hard I tried, it lay dormant inside me. Like my friends had just disappeared off the face of the earth.

Panic raced through me, acid burning my veins.

No, no. Get it together.

They weren't gone. There had to be magic in the mist that was blocking my dragon sense. That was a hundred times more likely than them just disappearing off the face of the earth. They were okay. All I had to do was find them.

I sucked in a shaky breath and tried to still my spinning mind. I took a few steps, hoping that the mist would clear ahead and I could use my dragon sense.

The ground dropped out from beneath me. My stomach jumped into my throat as I fell, sliding down the snowy mountainside. I scrabbled, trying to catch hold of something to still my fall. But I just kept sliding faster and faster, icy snow sneaking into my jacket as I hurtled.

I picked up speed until I slammed into a boulder that was almost entirely covered with snow.

Pain screamed through my leg, making tears spring to my eyes and bile rise in my throat. I sucked in a ragged breath and tried to get my bearings, but the mist was still thick down here.

Tentatively, I shifted my leg. Agony flared, worse than I'd ever felt before.

Broken?

Trembling, I tried to stand. It took all my strength to drag myself to my feet using the giant rock for support. By the time I was upright, sweat dampened my skin.

The moment I put pressure on my leg, it flared with gut-wrenching pain, and I stumbled to my knees. Icy ground met my palms, and I knelt in the snow, gasping.

This was bad.

A low growl sounded from behind me. I stiffened, goosebumps prickling my skin.

Slowly, my head light, I turned.

Two pairs of glowing red eyes peered out of the mist, stalking toward me. For a second, my heart leapt. Hellhounds! I was saved.

But no.

They didn't have the irises of flame that hellhounds possessed. No, these eyes were stark red. Their bodies began to appear out of the mist when they were only a dozen feet away.

Huge white wolves with shaggy fur, they were as tall as horses and elegant in a terrifying way. Unlike the friendly, rounded faces of the hellhounds, these dogs had sharply angled faces that complemented their long fangs.

I scrambled back, panting. I couldn't run. Not a chance.

So I called on my Phantom magic, letting it flow through me with an icy chill.

My limbs turned blue and transparent as the magic took over. The wolves hesitated at the sight, then prowled closer. I could hardly breathe as I dragged myself backward through the snow, away from them.

They stalked forward. When a massive paw landed on my uninjured leg and pinned me to the ground, I almost screamed.

He shouldn't be able to make contact with me in Phantom form! I wasn't protected.

Immediately, I pulled my sword from the ether and pointed the blade at the hound.

"One step closer…" I said.

The wolf growled, flaring its nostrils. Then it stopped abruptly, sniffing the air. The snarl faded from its face, and it bent to sniff my knee. Then a long tongue lolled out of its mouth and its eyes warmed.

Huh?

"Who are you?" I asked.

The wolf plopped its butt in the snow. The other sat beside it. They both grinned at me, massive white snow monsters on four legs. Trembling with the strain of adrenaline, I lowered the sword and reached out for their magic, trying to get a feel for what kinds of animals they really were. Because they were no ordinary wolves—not if they could touch me while I was in my Phantom form.

I got a hint of something familiar, though it was hard to define. The wolves didn't smell like brimstone like the hellhounds did, though I couldn't help but think they were some kind of Underworld wolf. Their magic had that feeling to it—like it was from another world. Or they walked between worlds.

"Do I know you guys?" I asked.

They just smiled.

Well, this had improved. I may have a broken leg and be lost in the mountains, but at least they weren't trying to eat me.

"Can you guys help me stand?" I asked.

They stayed seated, uncomprehending, so I shifted toward them and put a hand on the nearest one's back, struggling to stand. An involuntary cry escaped me when I put weight on my injured leg.

The closest dog's head whipped up toward me, concern clear in its red gaze. I'd always had an affinity for animals, but I'd never been able to identify outright concern in their gaze before. But these guys were special. Like Pond Flower.

I was the freaking Snow White of devil dogs, apparently.

The wolf looked down at my injured leg, sniffing it. I flinched when he pressed his nose to my shin, but the pain began to fade.

"What the heck?" I muttered.

The pain continued to dull, fading away to nothing. When the wolf removed his nose, I put my weight on the limb.

No pain. I tried a few steps. It worked just fine.

I turned back to the wolf, who sat a few feet away. His head was level with my chest. His buddy was identical, and though I couldn't see a difference between them, I could feel it. Their magic was slightly different.

"You healed me," I said. "Thank you."

The wolf just stared at me.

"Will you help me find my friends?" I didn't know what magic they were capable of, but if healing was in their repertoire, maybe understanding English and tracking were.

But the dogs did nothing.

Damn.

A few moments later, they stood and trotted away. They stopped after about ten feet, looking back at me expectantly.

"You want me to follow?"

They smiled toothily, though I didn't think they understood me.

I talked to them anyway. "I can't go that way." I pointed back up the hill. "My friends are that way."

They didn't move, so I waved and turned, starting the long climb up the hill. I sheathed my sword in the ether as I climbed, having to use my hands to scramble up the steep parts.

I followed the tracks I'd made when I'd tumbled down. Cold numbed my nose and chilled my lungs as the rest of me sweated up a storm in my snow gear. About halfway up, the two massive dogs joined me, plodding along like it was a walk in the park. By the time I made it back to the top, I was panting.

"Cass! Nix!" I squinted into the mist. "Roarke!"

Nothing.

Shit.

It wasn't unexpected, but disappointing anyway. I was going to have to get clever. If they couldn't hear me, maybe they could see me. I called on my magic, shifting into Phantom form and letting my blue glow light up the mist around me. It worked, a bit like how a car's headlights lit up the fog.

I chewed my lip as I waited.

Come on.

I squeezed my eyes closed and focused everything I had on trying to sense what was around me. The fresh scent of snow, the bite of the cold wind, the sound of nothingness. I prayed to hear footsteps.

Instead, I felt the strangest connection through the ice at my feet. Like it was alive almost. Strange. I'd never had that power before.

"Del!"

My heart leapt as my eyes popped open.

"Nix! Where are you?" I spun, searching the mist blindly.

A second later, Nix slammed into me. Shocked, I hugged her. She winced a bit at my Phantom touch, but didn't pull away. For some reason, it didn't hurt my *deirfiúr* as much as it hurt the demons I touched.

"How'd you find me?" I asked.

"Your blue glow! You're lit up like a beacon."

I grinned. "Awesome."

"Let's wait for the others. Maybe they'll see it too. What have you been doing all this time?" Her gaze dropped to my side and widened. She jumped back. I grabbed her hand before she could get too far, not wanting to lose her in the mist.

She pointed to the dogs. "Watch out!"

I glanced down at the dogs who sat at my side. "Oh, they're my friends."

"Yeah?"

I nodded and reached out to touch the head of the big white beast closest to me. His fur was icy soft. Not an ounce of warmth—not like you'd find on a real, living animal.

Definitely Underworld dogs.

"They helped me when I broke my leg," I said.

Nix's gaze darted down to my feet. "Are you okay?"

"They healed me. But where were you?"

"Wandering around this mountain." She glanced around. "It's been a while. I'd have thought they'd have found us by now."

"Me too." Worry niggled in my chest. This had been my only idea.

Except...

The snow below my feet still felt weird. Alive, almost. With energy.

"I'm going to try something." I called on my new ice power, letting the chill fill me. But instead of powering up an icicle, I focused on the ground below. The magic in the snow intensified, like a living thing. "I think I have some power over the snow. From the ice demon's gift that I stole."

Nix's brow wrinkled. "That makes sense. What can you do with it?"

"I don't know." I closed my eyes and focused on the magic beneath me. The ice felt like a living blanket—

which sounded weird, but it was the only way I could visualize it. Off to my left, I felt the tiniest bit of warmth.

"We need to walk." I moved toward the warmth, opening my eyes and walking across the snow while following the weird map within my mind. I pulled on Nix's hand and she followed. "I may feel them."

"Feel them?"

"Yeah."

The dogs went ahead of us, hopefully to scout it out and keep me from walking off a cliff. I held tight to Nix's hand, not wanting to lose her. The mist was so thick that I couldn't see an inch of the ground in front of me. As the dogs walked, I realized that the mist cleared around them, allowing me to see the snow.

"The dogs keep the mist away," I said.

"Thank magic."

"I'm definitely getting a better handle on my ice powers," I murmured as I followed the map in my mind. Occasionally I had to reach out and nudge one of the dogs' butts to keep them going in the direction I wanted, but they complied.

"Forced into it," Nix said. "Fastest way to learn."

"Ain't that the truth. And I've never been surrounded by so much snow." I focused on my magic, making sure not to lose my connection with the ice. "We're close."

A moment later, the dogs pulled up short. Ahead of them, two shadowy figures appeared out of the mist. Immediately, Aidan stepped between Cass and the dogs. She prodded him aside.

"Cass! Aidan!" I cried.

"Del!" Cass started to dart around the dogs, but Aidan threw out an arm and stopped her.

"Stop!" he said. "Those are the Cŵn Annwn. Wolves from the Welsh Underworld. But they're said to be deadly. They kill any trespassers on their land." His gaze met mine. "At least, they're supposed to. They seem to like you."

I reached down and scratched the head of the one nearest me. "I like them."

"Good. Because without you, they'd probably have eaten the rest of us."

"Eaten? They aren't that big," I said.

"But they're fierce," Aidan said. "My father used to tell me about them. They obey you, though."

"Kinda?" I scratched the other one's head. "They aren't going to kill anyone."

Aidan nodded and slowly lowered his arm. Cass walked around him and approached, throwing her arms around me, wincing slightly at my Phantom touch. "We were so worried."

"So was I." I released her. "We have to find Roarke."

Something bumped into me from behind. I stumbled forward. Strong arms reached around my waist. I stiffened before recognizing the touch.

"Roarke!" I spun to hug him.

Relief was stark in his gaze. "Are you all right?"

"Fine. How'd you find me?"

"Followed you. I can sense you, remember?"

Oh, right. He'd mentioned something about being able to do that. It was weird, but handy.

"Though I was held up when I walked off a mountainside," he added.

Thank fates it wasn't only me. That fog had been *thick*.

"Were you hurt?" I asked.

"No." He squeezed me tight to him, murmuring in my ear. "I'm glad you're all right."

"Me too." I returned the hug, then pulled back.

"Now what?" Nix asked.

Roarke gripped my hand. "Stick together."

"Hold hands and stay with the dogs." I called on my dragon sense, seeking my family's home base. It tugged at me, thank fates. "I can lead us there. But the dogs will make sure we can see each other through this mist."

Now that I'd found my friends, I let my Phantom glow fade. We joined hands in a line and began to walk, following the two hounds. The closer we drew, the faster they walked.

"I think the dogs know where we're going," Roarke said.

"Yeah. They must live here," I said.

"Does anyone else?" Aidan asked.

"I don't think so." I could feel no more warmth through the ice, like I had with Cass and Aidan. And Flora had said my family was dead.

The mist cleared abruptly. We all pulled up short, silenced by the sight ahead.

"Holy shit," Cass said. "This is your front door?"

"Are you sure you didn't grow up in *Lord of the Rings*?" Nix asked.

She had a point. It was pretty fantastical.

A massive stone bridge crossed a great gap in the mountain ahead. Ice coated the whole thing. At the other end, a massive stone wall hulked between two giant boulders. I caught glimpses of the fortress beyond. It was built into the mountain, making use of the outcroppings of rock.

No wonder my dreams of the past had been dreary.

"Let's go." I didn't want to dwell on anything except our goal. I released Nix's and Roarke's hands and started toward the bridge.

The dogs preceded me, looking right at home as they trotted over the ice bridge. I swallowed hard and followed, careful not to lose my footing. The gate at the other end was a monstrosity of wood and iron.

How the hell were we going to open that thing?

We moved silently across the bridge. Once, I almost lost my footing on the slick surface, but Roarke caught my arm.

When we reached the gate, the dogs stopped and looked up at me expectantly.

"What am I supposed to do?" I whispered to them.

They turned their gazes to the gate. I examined the ornately decorated surface, taking in the swirls and angles of the iron that coated the surface.

"Impressive workmanship." Nix reached out to touch a particularly swirly bit of metal. When her gloved fingertips made contact, the metal sizzled and she yelped, jumping back. "What the hell!"

"Did it burn you?" Cass demanded.

"Yeah."

I glanced at the wolves, whose gazes were still going back and forth between me and the gate. It was pretty clear what the wolves expected me to do.

Open the gate.

But how?

Warily, I glanced at Del, who was still shaking her hand to cool the burn. It'd burned right through her glove. But something inside me screamed to touch the gate. Tentatively, I reached a fingertip out and pressed it to the wood.

"Careful!" Cass cried as my fingertip made contact.

It didn't burn, so I moved my hand to the metal. That didn't burn either. It was just icy cold.

A memory flashed in my mind, something that had been locked up for a long time. Riding on a horse behind my father, crossing this bridge, and watching him press his hand flat to the big metal rose in the center of the gate. He glowed a bright blue in his Phantom form.

My heart thudded. This flash of memory was the first time I'd ever seen my father. He was a big man with a hard face and a long beard. Was he full Phantom or just half, like me?

His face faded from my mind almost as quickly as it'd appeared.

I called upon my Phantom form, letting the cold flow through me. Once I'd turned fully, I raised my hand. The rose looked out of place amongst all this ice, but I tried it, pressing my gloved hand to the flower.

Nothing happened. No burning, but it also didn't open. So I yanked off my glove and pressed my bare hand to the metal. Cold iced my palm, but magic sang up my arm.

A blue glow raced from the iron rose across all the swirls and straps of iron that decorated the gate. It glowed brilliantly for a moment before the metal and wood began to creak and groan.

"It's working!" Nix cried as the gate slowly lifted.

I removed my hand and stepped back, heart in my throat. Slowly, the massive gate opened to reveal a barren courtyard paved in gray stone. Ice dripped off the walls within, a creepy decoration for a place frozen in time. In the middle of the courtyard sat a large fountain that spewed frozen water. On the other side, a grand building sat, built into the mountainside. The glass windows were all blown out, and the gaping spots stood out starkly like blackened eyes.

Behind it to the left was a tower. My tower. A path led toward it. Answers would be there. I knew they would.

But we had to go through the main entrance. My dragon sense tugged that way.

"I think Draka may be here," I murmured. "Through the main door."

My dragon sense had picked her up as soon as we'd gotten close. I forced myself to step through the gate. Energy sparked through my veins as the residual magical power left in this place bombarded me.

"Feel that?" Cass whispered.

"Powerful magic," Aidan said.

"Decayed magic." Roarke parted his lips as if to taste the air.

He was right. It was just like the magic in the artifacts we found. Old and decayed. Abandoned.

"What happened to them all?" I whispered. Everyone who'd once lived here… They were all dead.

Cass and Nix each reached for one of my hands. I gripped theirs tightly and sucked in a ragged breath. However I'd ended up with the Monster when I was a teenager; maybe it had saved my life. Because whatever had befallen my parents' old stronghold—it'd taken everyone.

I could've tried to turn back time to see, but I didn't want to get caught in the middle of whatever had wiped them all out. Honestly, I was scared. I didn't want to witness the catastrophe that had taken this place.

And Draka waited. She needed us

"We need to move," Roarke said. "This place is abandoned, but the magic that remains here is dangerous."

He was right. I nodded and set off across the courtyard toward the building on the other side. As I walked, I thought I caught shimmers of something in the air. But when I turned my head, it was gone.

Going crazy.

But still… "I can't shake the feeling that we're not alone."

"Draka is here," Roarke said. "Is it her that you feel or something else?"

"I don't know."

Ahead of me, the wolves stiffened. Their big heads swung left, and their red eyes stared hard at the ice-covered wall. Their lips peeled back in a snarl, and deep growls rose up in their chests.

Instinctively, I called on my sword, drawing it from the ether. The blade glowed a bright cobalt, a slice of blue flame against our stark white and gray surroundings.

"What's coming?" Roarke asked.

I studied the wall. "I don't know."

"I feel it." Nix shuddered hard next to me. "Miserable."

The icy fortress wall glowed blue right before a dozen figures stepped forward.

Phantoms!

Strange joy leapt in my heart, snuffing into ashes when I noticed the black, soulless pits that were their eyes. These Phantoms weren't like me. They weren't my kin—not people who I could talk to and learn about my past.

No, they were monsters. Full-blooded Phantoms who existed off the misery of others.

I was half Phantom. And that made all the difference.

"Run!" I stepped toward the monsters and raised my blade.

Roarke stepped up beside me. "Hell no."

Slowly, they walked toward us. As if they had us trapped and had all the time in the world to enjoy the kill.

"You better do as she says, Roarke," Nix muttered as she backed away from the Phantoms who approached. "She's fought off more than this on her own. You can't fight them. One touch and you'll be crippled by the pain. There's nothing you can do against them."

Nix was right. We'd tried fighting them off together this summer. My friends' weapons had done nothing to the Phantoms. Only my blade could touch them.

"Go!" I waved her toward the building we'd been heading for. "If the Phantoms get ahold of you guys, we're screwed."

"See ya!" Cass said. "You've got this."

I so did. I'd fought off twice this many that past summer. But Roarke wasn't following the others toward the building.

"Seriously, Roarke," I said. "You're a liability. Only a Phantom can hurt another Phantom. They're full blooded Phantoms. If they touch you, it'll be agony."

They were almost on us. Only a dozen feet away.

"I'll be fine." The gray tornado of mist surrounded him as he shifted to his demon form. His magic filled the air with the scent of sandalwood that was rich against the cold, crisp breeze.

My gaze darted between him and the approaching Phantoms. They were dressed in clothes from all periods, so it was impossible to tell what era they'd come from. But every single one had that same ravenous black gaze.

It shouldn't surprise me that my home was full of these things, but it made a prickle of fear race down my spine.

What other miseries did this place hide?

"Please, Roarke, go!" I stepped toward the Phantoms, my blade raised.

He said nothing. Just stepped up beside me. I spared him one last anguished glance, praying I could kill the Phantoms before they got to him, then raced toward my prey.

They crowded around me, drawn by…something. I didn't know why they went for me and not Roarke, but I was grateful.

I lunged at the nearest one, a middle-aged man dressed like a farmer, and swiped out with my sword. It cut through his neck as if his blue flesh were made of butter, separating his head from his body. The thing tumbled off and bounced. I leapt aside and thrust my blade into the gut of a woman who reached for me with clawed hands.

For a moment, I almost hesitated.

Because being around them felt *good*. Just like it had last time.

I shuddered, hating that, and spun to face the next Phantom, removing its arm in an easy strike. Its black gaze darted to mine and guilt flared.

Was I killing my own kind?

What kind of monster was I?

From the corner of my eye, I saw three of the Phantoms split off, heading for my friends, who were nearly to the main entrance of the fortress. The evil hunger in the Phantoms' gazes hardened my heart.

I'd chosen my family. Cass, Nix, and now Aidan. Maybe Roarke.

Either way, I wouldn't let these monsters have them.

I fought with everything I had, taking out two more Phantoms, desperate to reach the ones who were heading for my friends.

But Roarke cut them off, reaching for them with his massive, clawed hands. Before I could scream at him not to touch them, he grabbed one and broke its neck.

I did a double take, my jaw slack.

How the hell had he gotten ahold of one? His touch should have sailed right through them. A phantom slammed into me from behind, locking its arms around me.

Shit!

I thrashed, trying to break free. To anyone else, it would seem like the Phantom was hugging me. But Phantoms fought by embracing their victims. Their touch ignited the magic that sent their prey into a mental tailspin of misery and pain, which the Phantoms fed off of. I could do it with my own touch, though I didn't feed off another's pain like the Phantoms did.

The Phantom's grip slackened—he was probably surprised that I *liked* his touch. I used the chance to break free of his grip and spun around. My gaze caught my enemy's right before I plunged my blade into his gut.

Guilt flared within me as I yanked the sword free. I thought I saw shock in his eyes, but that wasn't possible. They were just dark holes.

"Behind you, Del!" Nix cried from the other side of the courtyard.

I clearly didn't have time for an existential crisis.

I spun to face the two Phantoms who closed in on me. With a swipe of my sword, I took the head from one. The other got a grip on my arm, but I shoved my blade deep into his gut. He doubled over, and I yanked the steel free, gagging slightly.

Fighting normally didn't bother me, but something about hurting the Phantoms—even though I knew they were evil—was making me queasy.

The transparent blue bodies were scattered around me and slowly disappearing. All were fallen. Roarke had taken out five.

"How the hell did you manage that?" I demanded.

His gray wings were flared wide at his back, and he glanced up, his gaze dark. "I'm the Warden of the Underworld. Phantoms are in my wheelhouse."

"Did you know that before right now?"

He grinned, his teeth stark white in his dark face. "No."

"Never turned away from a fight, huh?"

He shook his head. "Not yet."

Not ever, I'd bet. "Let's go."

I turned and started toward the main house. My friends stood in the doorway. The white wolves followed me, but stopped about ten feet from the door.

"You leaving?" I asked them.

They gave me one last look, then turned and walked back toward the entrance to the compound.

I turned toward my friends. Cass nodded at the disappearing blue bodies of the Phantoms and asked, "Who the heck were they?"

"I don't know. Weird relatives?" I said. Everyone else got to have an aunt who pinched their cheeks or an uncle who liked his rifles too much. Me? I got soul-sucking Phantoms.

"Well, your parents were loaded." Nix stepped back and swept her arm into the main part of the house.

The breath whooshed out of me. It was the fanciest, most beautiful foyer I'd ever seen. The grim exterior of the fortress gave way to a mansion of incredible proportions. The interior was done entirely in shades of white, gray, and black, but somehow it didn't feel as cold as it should. It was still chilly, but not terrible.

The main hall was the size of a football field, with glittering chandeliers hanging from the ceiling at regular intervals. Ice dripped from the crystals, making them sparkle even more in the dim sunlight that filtered in through the broken windows. The floor was a mosaic of beautiful stone tiles, and the walls were covered with artwork. Enchantments must've protected the paintings, because they were the only color in the room and the only things that hadn't been coated by ice.

"This place is nuts," I muttered.

"Recognize anything?" Nix asked.

"Nope." My chest tightened with loss. I hadn't thought about it much, but what I'd wanted to do was walk in and feel at home.

But of course I felt nothing. My only memories were of being locked in a tower with just Draka for company. So yeah, fun childhood memories were probably not going to come crashing at me.

When my eyes started to prickle with tears, I looked immediately at Cass and Nix.

The tears dried right up.

I had family now. The best friends a girl could ask for. An amazing job and even a hot boyfriend-like dude in my life.

Whatever miserable memories this mausoleum held for me didn't matter. They were gone, and that was in the past. My future was bright.

My gaze caught on one of the bright paintings on the wall.

Heck, maybe I could fence the art. Sell this place to make a creepy *Haunted Mansion*-themed ski resort.

There were positives here, damn it, and I was going to find them.

"You okay?" Cass murmured with a knowing gaze. She'd been through this, too, though it'd been different.

I smiled at her. "Yeah. We're close to Draka. I can feel it."

I hadn't been sure if she'd be here, but this was good.

"Then let's go."

We made our way silently across the foyer, following my dragon sense. Aidan and Roarke flanked our little group, and while I appreciated the protective instincts, I wasn't sure it was necessary. Not only could we three handle whatever came at us, this place felt empty and cold as the grave.

Not that that meant anything in the Kingdom of the Dead.

Because if I was Death in the Triumvirate and this place was full of Phantoms, I couldn't think of anything else to call my home.

On the other side of the foyer, a pair of massive wooden doors stood closed. They gleamed dark and beautiful in the dim gray light.

Roarke stopped in front of them and turned to me. "Do you want me to open them?"

"No, but thank you. I have to do this." Even though I didn't think I wanted to, because the whole place gave me the creeps. How he'd sensed that, I had no idea.

He stepped aside and I approached, pressing my hands to the cold wood. I could feel everyone's gazes as I pushed the doors open.

A whoosh of cold air rushed up from below, blowing me back a step. I coughed and blinked.

"Whoa." Nix leaned through the doorway and peered down the stairs.

I looked too. A massive spiral staircase led down far, far into the ground. The thing had to be at least twenty feet across. A regimen of soldiers could troop up and down. The fact that they went down was weird, though. I wouldn't have thought we were on the top floor.

"Some dungeon," Cass muttered.

"I don't think it is a dungeon." I had no memories of this place, but it was far too nice to be a dungeon. "There are no stairs leading up and no other doors off this room, so the rest of the"—I had no idea what to call this place—"fortress must be downstairs."

No one would ever call this place a *house*. It was a fortress, through and through.

I stepped down onto the first stair, then made my way silently into the chill below. My friends followed,

Roarke at my side. I kept my blade gripped in my hand as we walked and maintained my Phantom form.

"Long way down," Nix whispered.

"Yeah." We had to have gone at least three stories, but I couldn't say for sure. My skin prickled with awareness as we trod silently downward. "But we're closer to Draka."

Another large room spread out at the base of the stairs. It was high ceilinged and empty, with gray stone vaults above. Large doors broke up the wall on the far side. There were rugs on the floor where furniture may have been grouped once, but it was long gone. Though we were underground and there were no windows, the stone itself glowed with a pale light, enough to illuminate the large space.

"Enchanted stone?" Cass asked.

Aidan walked to the nearest wall and laid his hand on the faintly glowing stone. "No. Not enchanted by a supernatural, at least. I think the stone itself is magic."

"Catalight," Roarke said. "We have it in the Underworld."

"Why does that not surprise me?" I said. Of course my Phantom father would have something like this. I didn't know what exactly our relationship to the Underworld was, but it was weird.

"It should," Roarke said. "This stuff shouldn't be able to glow like this on Earth. I don't know how it does."

Unease prickled across my skin.

A crash sounded from another room. I stiffened, glancing at my friends. They were still as statues, listening, but we didn't hear anything else.

Let's go, I mouthed.

We crept across the stone floor silently. When I reached the door on the other end, I took a deep breath and eased it open. Again, the room within was large.

But there was a throne on the other side. A freaking throne made of silver and thorns. Beside it, Draka sat in her human form, bound with a heavy iron chain. The room was otherwise empty.

I gasped, then raced inside, hurrying toward her.

Her gaze darted up, meeting mine. Panic flared in her eyes. She threw out a hand as if to stop me. "No! Go back!"

Confusion ricocheted through me, but I raced ahead, desperate to get to her. She was alone. I could free her, and we could run for it.

In the middle of the room, electricity zapped through me, but I kept going, barely noticing that the light changed a bit on this side of the room. A half second later, demons spilled out from the walls. Dozens of them, coming right out of the stone. I skidded to a halt, raising my blade in front of me.

Where the hell had they been hiding?

Magic vibrated in the air. Concealment charm. But no one had felt it when we'd first stepped in the door—and we would've definitely felt something like this. There were demons of all species armed with all manner of weapons.

Cass and Nix screamed from behind me, rage and frustration sharp in their voices. Why weren't they at my side?

As the horde of demons closed in on me, I glanced quickly behind to see my *deirfiúr*. They'd only made it halfway across the room and were beating their fists against an invisible barrier. Aidan had transformed into a griffon, but was trapped on that side, too. Roarke was drawing back his fist to try to slam through the barrier.

Shit.

Somehow, I'd gone through a portal.

"Run!" Draka screamed. "It's a trap!"

Shit.

I turned back. There were at least two dozen demons, with more still coming. They headed straight for me. I called upon my ice magic, letting it fill me with its chill. I hurled a spear of ice at the nearest demon with enough force that it sailed straight through his abdomen and pierced the chest of another demon. They both dropped hard to the floor.

I created the icicles as fast as I could and threw them at any demon who neared.

A demon with transparent blue skin—one who looked almost like a Phantom except for his horns— threw a flaming ball of fire toward me. It sailed at my legs.

Instinctually, I lunged out of the way, even though it shouldn't have been able to hurt me while I was in my Phantom form. Before I could conjure an icicle, the demon hurled another ball of blue flame at me.

I wasn't quick enough this time. The fiery ball slammed into my upper thigh. Burning pain flared through me.

What the hell?!

It should have sailed right through me. But whatever species this demon was, its magic could affect me. Was it some kind of Phantom demon?

It maintained its distance as the other demons charged me. A tall demon neared, and I went corporeal long enough to plunge my blade into its huge stomach. As I was drawing the steel free, the Phantom demon hurled another fire bomb.

I wasn't fast enough to dodge this one either. The flame hit my left knee. I stumbled, but righted myself just as a great crash sounded. Magic rippled through the air. A moment later, Roarke swept through the air beside me, picking up a demon who had jumped for me and hurling it against the wall.

Half the demons in the room stopped dead still at the sight of Roarke, now on their side of the barrier. I heard fearful whispers of 'the Warden' before a dozen of them turned tail and ran, disappearing through the door on the far side of the room, behind Draka.

But there were still so many. And my burns were making me slow.

"Your friends can't make it through the barrier!" Roarke yelled. "We're outnumbered!"

He'd made it through because he was Warden of the Underworld, but they couldn't cross. I stole a glance at them.

"Retreat!" Cass screamed, gesturing wildly. "There are too many!"

"No!" I couldn't. Draka was still chained.

A big hand grabbed my shoulder and I spun. Before I could turn corporeal and thrust my blade, my demon attacker slammed his hand against my chest and delivered an electric shock that threw me through the air.

I crashed to my back, stunned.

Adrenaline kicked into high gear, and I blinked frantically to regain my vision. Before I could rise, the demon who'd attacked me leapt upon me. I threw him off me and charged up my ice power.

He fell to his side, and I leapt on him, sending a bolt of ice straight into his chest. I had a split second's thought that I should steal his power, but I shoved it away and leapt back.

It might have been stupid to let that deadly power go to waste when I could have made it my own, but I couldn't risk it. What side effects would come with it? What if I couldn't control those?

Fear made me back off, unwilling to take the power.

"Get out of there!" Cass screamed.

I spun to face my next attacker, but my burned legs made me awkward and slow. In the air, Roarke tore the head off a demon, then met my gaze.

More demons were appearing. We were holding off the ones nearest to us, but there were *so* many. Nearly forty now.

"We can't fight them all," Roarke yelled. He grabbed a demon by one massive horn and threw him away from me.

"Go!" Draka screamed.

We were so outnumbered.

I gave her one last agonized glance. "We'll come back!"

Before I could turn, a massive demon grabbed me around the waist and heaved me over his shoulder. An enraged shriek escaped me as I stabbed him in the lower back.

Before he could collapse and take me to the ground with him, Roarke grabbed me, sweeping me up in his arms. He hurtled toward the barrier, powerful wings keeping us above the heads of the demons, who roared their rage and followed.

"Go!" Roarke yelled. "I weakened the barrier. They may make it through."

My friends turned and ran, racing across the room and through the doors. Roarke set me on the ground so I could run, and we followed my friends, leaving the demons behind.

Just as my friends couldn't cross the barrier, the demons couldn't either. I glanced back to see them beating their fists against the invisible barrier, rage in their eyes. They might break through, they might not. But I didn't want to be here to find out.

We sprinted up the wide spiral staircase behind Nix, Cass, and Aidan, then across the massive great hall and out into the cold. My legs ached where the burns had eaten into my skin.

"Can you transport us out of here?" I yelled to Cass.

She hesitated briefly, her magic flaring. "No! I'm blocked."

"We need a cemetery," Roarke said. "Or a place that is haunted. I can create an Underpath."

"What about the courtyard where we killed all the Phantoms?" I asked.

"Could work."

We ran for it, skidding to a halt in the place that had been haunted by the Phantoms when we first came in. Roarke pulled back his fist and slammed it into the air, creating an Underpath entrance.

He grabbed my hand, and before I could open my mouth, he tugged me into the ether, leaving my friends behind.

CHAPTER SEVEN

We appeared a moment later in the woods by his house. I tugged away and spun to face him.

"Go back for them!" I yelled.

He gave me a look that could only be interpreted to mean *duh*, then stepped back through the portal. I paced while I waited, losing control of my Phantom form and turning corporeal. It was partially nerves, partially fear. The burns on my thighs were killing me.

It was only a few seconds before Roarke appeared with Nix. He let go of her hand and stepped back through the portal.

"Are you all right?" Nix hurried to me and knelt to look at my legs.

"Great."

"You don't look great." She winced. "Those burns look bad."

I eyed the portal worriedly, trying to ignore the pain. Roarke stepped through with Cass, then returned for Aidan.

"Handy skill he has there," Cass said.

"Yeah."

"He also made it through the barrier back at the castle," Nix said. "We couldn't break through."

"It had to be an Underworld portal or something," I said. "We're the only two who can cross them."

Roarke appeared with Aidan.

My shoulders relaxed. "Had the demons made it past the barrier?"

"Not yet." Roarke's gaze dropped to my legs. "We need to get you medical attention."

"I can do a bit of healing," Aidan said. "But she may need more care."

"What kind of fire was that, anyway?" Nix asked. "It hurt you while you were in your Phantom form."

"I don't know." Exhaustion hit me. The memory of the hike up the mountain, nearly drowning, the broken leg, and the strange demon fire sucked out every ounce of strength. My friends didn't look much better, honestly. "Roarke's place is really close. Can we have a shower and some food, then do a breakdown?"

"Yes." Cass's voice was emphatic.

"Let me heal your legs a bit to help with the pain." Aidan's gaze met Roarke's. "Then perhaps you could call your demon healer to finish what I can't."

Roarke nodded and pulled his phone from his pocket. "Thank you."

I stood still while Aidan hovered his hand over the burns. Comforting warmth flowed through me, and the pain faded slightly.

Aidan straightened. "That's the best I can do."

"Thank you." I glanced down to see that the flesh looked a bit better, but still like a barbecued chicken. The idea made me gag slightly.

Roarke lowered his phone. "Let's get back to my place. Lofta, the healer, will be there soon."

In silence, we walked through the woods.

"Fates, I'm beat," Nix muttered.

"Me too." My limbs felt like they were made of lead. When we finally climbed the steps onto Roarke's porch and made it inside, I was ready to sleep for a week.

I took a seat on the couch to wait for the healer while Roarke showed everyone to guest bedrooms where they could get cleaned up. The healer arrived while he was upstairs, letting herself into the house. She was the same one who always came to my aid when Roarke called her.

"You're the one I'm here to see?" the tiny demon asked as she approached. Her horns were small, but visible, and though she looked like a middle-aged woman, she clearly was not.

"Yeah, thanks for coming." I started to stand, but she waved me down.

"What've we got?" she asked.

"Burns."

"Nasty ones, too, from the look of them." She knelt at my side and hovered her gnarled hands over the burns. They faded quickly, and the pain followed, making me sag with relief.

"Thank you."

"Of course."

I was about to stand when she reached for my hand, gripping it tightly. Startled, I sought her gaze.

"What?"

"You're special." Her voice was fierce. "I don't know how, but you are. I can feel it in you. You are meant to accomplish great things."

"Like what?"

"I don't know. But I do know that people who are meant to accomplish great things often die while trying. Don't."

"Um, thank you for caring?" I wasn't sure what to say to that, but I didn't want to offend the healer, not after the many times she'd helped me.

"It's not for you," she whispered. "It's for Roarke. He's been alone a long time. He doesn't trust easily."

"I've noticed."

"Yes, well, he seems to have taken a liking to you. Don't leave him."

"I wouldn't." Wouldn't I? I didn't know.

A sardonic smile pulled at the corner of her mouth. "When I say don't *leave* him, I mean don't fail at your fated task. That will tear two you apart."

I swallowed hard. "I'll definitely try not to do that."

She nodded sharply and stood. "Good luck with your task."

Before I could ask what the hell she knew about my task, she turned and left.

But then, I had a feeling she'd have told me more if she'd known. She really didn't want me to fail. Not for my sake, nor for the sake of the world. But for Roarke.

He appeared in the living room a moment later. He was so handsome and good and strong that I could see why Lofta had given him her loyalty.

"Did Lofta come?" he asked.

I stood, finally pain free for the first time since I'd been burned. "Yes. She fixed me right up."

He approached, gently gripping my shoulders. His dark gaze was concerned when it met mine. Pained. "I was so damned worried when those demons charged you and I was on the other side of the barrier."

He looked so torn up. Like he really, truly cared about me. My heart thudded. I didn't know what to say, so I stood on my tiptoes and pressed my lips to his. He groaned low in his throat and cupped the back of my head, kissing me like his life depended on it.

After too short a time, he pulled away. "I'm going to order Thai if you want to get cleaned up."

"Okay." I stepped back, then made my way upstairs. I glanced back right before I reached the top.

Roarke was watching me, a hundred different expressions on his face that I couldn't identify.

And the thing was, I thought I felt a hundred different things for him. And I had no idea what to do about that.

By the time I finished my shower and made it back downstairs, I was feeling more alive. Nix and Cass were sitting on the living room couch in front of the fire, both dressed in PJs that I assumed Nix had conjured.

With the rustic chic surroundings, they looked like they'd just gotten off the slopes instead of the mess we'd just been through.

"Burns all better?" Cass asked.

"Yeah. How're you guys?"

Nix sipped a mug of something that steamed, then sighed and said, "Much better."

"Same." Cass handed me her mug. "Try this. It's excellent."

I took a sip and grinned. Spiced wine. It tasted like warm, sweet Christmas in a mug. "Where are the guys?"

"In the kitchen, chatting about manly stuff. Thai food should be here soon."

My stomach grumbled.

"Hey, why didn't you take that demon's electricity power?" Cass asked.

The question was so out of the blue that I almost spilled the wine.

"What do you mean?" I asked.

"I saw you hesitate." Cass's gaze was concerned. "You were in a life or death situation, and you could have had a power that would light up any jerk who touched you. But you didn't take it. You should have taken it."

I lowered the wine, my heart pounding. "Of course I couldn't take it. What about the side effects?"

"Of what? Zapping people? I know you had a bad run-in with the Ubilaz demon's power, but he's an anomaly. Most powers are simpler. Helpful. You need all the help you can get."

My mind raced. She had a point, and I knew it. But I was afraid. And being called out on that fear sucked.

"I know what you mean," I said. "But we've spent so many years fighting our FireSoul natures and not stealing powers that it's second nature for me not to do that. And I'm not like you, Cass. You have experience taking powers. You've learned to control them. What if I can't control them like you do?"

She reached for my arm and gave me a squeeze. The love in her gesture calmed me a bit.

"I was a mess, too, remember?" Cass said. "I was afraid of my magic, and that got me nowhere. But I fumbled my way through my changing powers. You will, too."

"I agree with Cass," Nix said. "You have something big coming. I know you're afraid you can't handle it... Or handle the new powers that keep cropping up, but you can. I know you can."

"And you have to," Cass said.

I nodded. "I know. I thought of taking his power, but I freaked out. Next time, maybe I will."

"If it's a power that could help you, then I think you definitely should," Cass said. "You need a stronger arsenal to fight whatever is coming."

The doorbell rang, and Roarke strode out of the kitchen. I caught his gaze briefly and he smiled, then went to collect the food.

I was famished by the time the cartons and silverware were laid out on the table. So was everyone else, apparently. We each grabbed a plastic container at random and dug in.

As we ate with the fire crackling in the background, I couldn't help but be grateful for my friends. I swallowed a mouthful of noodles and said, "Thanks for all the help today, guys. We never would have made it without you."

"No' a problem," Cass said around a mouthful. "We're a team."

I grinned. We finished eating, then sat back, satisfied. I wished we really were at a ski resort instead of facing the problems we were facing.

But then I realized that was a lie. I didn't want Draka to be held captive, but I liked the challenge ahead of me. I'd always thrived on this type of thing. I might've doubted myself sometimes, but I always threw myself back in it.

"So, how about that elephant in the room?" Nix said. "Because that was clearly a trap."

I nodded. "Yeah. I think those demons forced Draka to make the connection with me that told me where she was. That's why there were failed attempts in the beginning—with the blue light that never quite made the connection."

"Like that episode in Honduras and at Emile's party."

I nodded, thinking of the moment when the flash of blue light in my mind had disabled me.

"They want you for something, but they must not be able to find you," Roarke said. "So they're drawing you to them with Draka as bait."

"Or they can't get past that barrier," Nix said.

"Yeah." I sipped the spiced wine that had cooled. "Flora said my old home is between the Underworld and Earth. That must be what she means."

"Do you think they want you because you're part of the Triumvirate?" Cass asked.

"Or because you have weird death powers?" Nix added.

"Maybe both."

"You need answers," Roarke said. "There are too many unknowns, and that makes this situation more dangerous."

"Yeah. We walked into a trap today," I said.

As much as I wanted to run straight back there to get Draka, we couldn't fight off those demons if we just repeated our actions. Not if we couldn't bring Cass, Nix, and Aidan through the barrier to help us fight. "We need another way to get to Draka."

"And answers about your past," Aidan said. "It has to all be linked. They didn't take her to your home just because it was partially in the Underworld. That place is important."

I nodded, remembering the feeling of walking through the courtyard and being desperate to explore. Particularly the tower out back.

"I need to go back," I said. "There are answers there. And maybe I can find another way to reach Draka that doesn't force me into their trap."

"We'll come with," Cass said.

I opened my mouth to tell her not to, but shut it again. She wouldn't listen. Just like I wouldn't listen to her if I thought she needed my help.

CHAPTER EIGHT

"Hey, wake up." I nudged Roarke in the side.

He groaned and rolled over, his broad chest nearly squishing me against the soft mattress. After dinner, we'd all crashed, too exhausted to stay up a moment longer. I'd curled up next to him, briefly considered climbing on top of him, then passed out before I'd finished the thought.

But it was now four a.m., and my plan needed to get a move on.

"Wake up!" I poked Roarke in the side.

He grunted and opened his eyes. "What time is it?"

"Early. But we need to sneak out of here before the others wake up. I'm not taking them into a trap. Not when our main goal is just recon."

He nodded, sitting up and scrubbing his hand over his hair. He looked so damned good that my palms itched to touch him.

"You're right," he said. "And we'll be quicker and quieter if it's just the two of us."

"Exactly." Though I felt bad for ditching them, it was for the best. As long as those demons were there, threatening to break past the barrier, it was too dangerous. The only escape route was through Roarke's Underpath, and he could only take one person at a time.

My friends had helped us get to the fortress—had been invaluable—but this time, I had to do this alone. If I hadn't needed Roarke to give me a lift through the Underpath, I'd have ditched him, too.

We dressed quickly, then snuck out of the house as quiet as thieves. Fortunately, Roarke's electric car was silent as he turned it on and drove us down the driveway. We were headed into town to pick up some invisibility potions from Connor. When we went back this time, I wanted to be fully prepared. If there were any demons wandering around my parents' old place, I didn't want them spotting us.

"You sure he'll be up this early?" Roarke asked as he drove down the darkened street. Tall trees loomed on either side.

"He's a baker. Of course he's up this early." I'd texted him last night just to be sure, though.

We pulled up to Potions & Pastille's twenty minutes later. The streets of Magic's Bend had been empty. The main lights in the restaurant were dim, but the door to the kitchen was open and it glowed with light.

I climbed out of Roarke's car, went to the front door, and tapped on the glass. Connor's head poked out the kitchen door a moment later. He grinned and hurried toward me to open the door wide.

"I left the music off so I'd hear you," he said.

"Thanks." I grinned and stepped inside.

Today, he wore a purple T-shirt with the band name Peatbog Faeries on it. White flour dusted his hands and sprinkled on his hair.

He nodded to Roarke. "Morning."

Roarke stepped inside the cafe. "Thanks for meeting us so early."

"Not a problem. Come on in. I'll get you the potions."

We followed him through the shop and into the kitchen, weaving through the narrow space to the door at the back. I hovered outside his tiny workshop, peering in. Unlike the kitchen, which was immaculate, the potions workshop was the lair of a mad scientist. It was cluttered with herbs, bottles of all colors, cauldrons, and little metal tools.

It was fabulous.

Connor poked around, grabbed a couple vials, then turned to us and handed over the potions. "Drink these when you want to become invisible. It should last several hours. You'll be able to see each other, but no one should be able to see you."

We were planning on the demons still being trapped on the other side of the barrier below the main throne room, but just in case, these would come in handy.

I took them. "Thank you."

Roarke nodded his thanks, and we followed Connor out through the kitchen and into the main cafe.

"And now for the coffee!" Connor clapped his hands together once and headed for the espresso machine.

"You're a hero."

The gleaming silver espresso machine steamed and hissed as he made us our beverages. He got us two paper cups and a bag of muffins.

"They're a day old since it's so early, but still tasty." Connor handed them over.

"Thank you. You're the best." I hugged him goodbye, then followed Roarke to the car.

"Let's use the Underpath near Mad Mordecai's in town so that we don't run into the others. I'll text them right before we go through so that they don't worry." I sipped the coffee, which tasted like hot, rich glory.

"Good idea." Roarke made quick work of getting to the Historic District. It helped that the streets were empty this time of morning.

I polished off the last of the muffin and espresso, then reached into the back seat and grabbed my puffy winter jacket. Just thinking about what we were heading into made me shiver. Roarke grabbed his own jacket, and I followed him out of the car.

As we hurried across the street, he reached for my hand. My fingertips curled around his as sparks shot up my arm.

"Are you doing all right?" he asked.

From his tone of voice, he clearly didn't mean, "Have you had enough for breakfast?" or anything similarly inane.

"Yeah." Actually, I was scared to death of what I might learn about my family. About myself.

"Liar."

I laughed softly. "Fine. I'm scared. That fortress is a terrible place. So cold and horrible. Not just because it's in those icy mountains. I can feel it. And there were Phantoms there. Full-blooded Phantoms."

"You're half Phantom, so it's not surprising they would be there."

"I know. But they're terrible creatures." I had a really bad feeling about my parents. I needed to know more, but I didn't think I wanted to.

"But *you're* not terrible," Roarke said.

"High praise."

He stopped, turning me to him. I met his gaze.

"I believe in you, Del." His voice was serious.

I wanted to crack a joke, but couldn't. He really did believe in me. He believed in me so much that he'd given up what he held most dear—abiding by the law. He should have turned me in to the Order of the Magica or dragged me back to hell. But he hadn't. Instead, he was at my side.

As much as I doubted myself sometimes—my dragon sense, my ability to control new powers—he didn't doubt me. Neither did my *deirfiúr*.

That alone gave me strength.

I smiled at him, reaching up to stroke his cheek. "Thank you, Roarke." I leaned up and pressed a quick kiss to his lips. "Now let's go kick some butt."

He grinned. "That's the spirit."

I stepped back and headed for the alley, pulling my little vial of potion from my pocket. Roarke did the same. We met each other's gazes, then pulled the corks out of the vials.

I held mine up. "Cheers."

He clinked his against mine, then we both swigged the bright blue liquid.

I gagged, forcing myself to swallow the disgusting, mud-flavored liquid. I'd never eaten mud, but I was one thousand percent sure this was what it tasted like.

Cold flowed through me, like when I turned into a Phantom. But the numbness that followed was unusual.

I reaching for Roarke's hand, and we stepped in front of the Underpath entrance. I couldn't see it, but we'd used it enough that I knew just where to stand. Fortunately, Roarke had created and Underpath entrance at the fortress in Wales, so we'd be able to get right in.

"Ready?" Roarke asked.

"Like a cat's ready for tuna."

Hand in hand, we stepped through the Underpath entrance. The ether sucked me in, and my head spun like a merry-go-round. Gravity lost all meaning for the briefest moment, then we stepped out into the cold, bright light of the Welsh morning.

I tensed, gaze darting around for enemies, but saw no one. No Phantoms. We must have killed them all.

"We're alone," Roarke said.

"Good." I trusted Connor's potion, but there were other ways for supernaturals to sense a person.

The fortress's grand, main entrance loomed on the left. I'd guess that it had been the formal visitor's entrance to my parents' *home,* though it was honestly hard to think of such a cold place as a home. But that way led straight down into the throne room.

Beside the main entrance was the winding path that led to the back of the compound. It had called to me on our last visit and still did.

I pointed toward it. "That way. I think it's the living quarters."

Roarke nodded and set off down the stone path. The cold wind nipped at my cheeks as we hurried along. The massive exterior wall soared to our left and buildings to our right.

Roarke hiked a thumb toward them. "Any of these have potential?"

"No." I felt nothing from them, though memories hovered at the edges of my mind. "We have to go to the tower."

It loomed ahead, like something Rapunzel would want to jump out of. The tower called to me, and I wasn't sure if it was my dragon sense or just my desire to visit the only place I remembered.

"I'm so tempted to bring this place back to life," I murmured. "Just to see what was here."

Roarke reached for my hand and squeezed.

We were nearly to the tower when a shuffling noise made me stiffen.

I nudged Roarke and he nodded. We pressed ourselves against the wall, standing dead still and silent.

A moment later, a demon appeared at the end of the path.

So some of the demons could get past the barrier. Not good.

I filed the information away for later.

The demon ambled down the walk, his big steps landing hard on the stone. He was the pale gray of an ice demon, the same type I'd stolen my power from.

I met Roarke's gaze and mouthed, *I've got this*.

He nodded once, and I turned back to the demon. As he approached, his eyes never swayed toward us, even though we stood right out in the open.

Clearly, Connor's potion worked.

I called upon my ice power. Hit him with a shot of his own medicine. I was almost fully charged for a massive icicle when his step faltered. He was still about twenty feet away, but his nose twitched.

My heart jumped in my chest. He smelled us.

The demon opened his mouth to shout. I had no more time, so I hurled the icicle, aiming straight for his head. It pierced him through the eye. Blood spurted around the white spear, a grisly sight.

The demon was dead in an instant, keeling over onto his front. The icicle shattered against the stone.

"Nicely done," Roarke murmured.

"Thanks." I hurried to the body and knelt, patting him down to see if he had any transportation charms or other useful goodies. I found nothing.

Annoyed, I stood. He was already starting to disappear, thank magic. The pathway was so barren that there wasn't anywhere good to hide him.

"Hopefully he'll be gone before anyone stumbles across him," Roarke said.

I knocked on my head, then started toward the tower that had once held me prisoner.

We reached the base a few moments later, and I tilted my head back, peering up. The slick gray stone would have made it impossible for anyone to climb the tower.

The perfect prison.

I walked around the side and found the wooden door, then tried to push it open. It stuck fast. I stepped back and studied it, noting the carving of a hand near the handle.

Tentatively, I laid my palm in the indentation. Nothing happened. Just the faint fizz of the charm that had been placed on the door.

"Let me." Roarke laid his hand where mine had been, then removed it. "The charm is keyed up to a certain person."

"My parents, most likely." The thought made my heart clutch.

"I'll take care of it." Roarke pulled his fist back and slammed it through the door. Magic vibrated out from the blow, and the wood disintegrated, falling to the ground as sawdust.

"Nice," I murmured, then hurried up the stairs.

The steps were narrow as they wound up, the sort that would keep attackers from easily swinging their sword as they climbed. This would have been the retreat of last resort during an attack.

Had my parents been trying to protect me by keeping me in here?

Somehow, I doubted it.

I reached the top where another wooden door blocked my way. This one opened to my touch, however, and I slipped inside.

Memories slammed into me as soon as I stepped across the familiar threshold. I didn't even have to bring this place back to life—the memories came, unbidden.

I was thirteen again, standing with my sword at my side. My skills were improving, but I still wasn't good enough. My magic… That languished.

Slowly, I turned to face the door. Instead of Roarke, my parents stood there. They were both tall and slender, with hawk-like appearances that were more a product of their bearing than their actual physical appearance.

They were birds of prey in human form. Even their dark eyes looked like they were constantly searching for their next target.

"Mother? Father? What brings you here?" Though I spoke, the words weren't mine. They were the words of my younger self.

I was having some kind of surreal flashback—like I'd morphed with my younger self—though why it delivered me to this moment, I had no idea.

"Delphine." My mother stepped into the room but didn't approach any closer. Her eyes traveled over me, assessing.

Finding me wanting.

My heart fell, the most visceral sensation of grief.

I'd seen her so infrequently in my life, but every time… Every single time… I'd hoped that she might suddenly change.

She did not change.

She would never change.

"You're going away," she said.

"Away?" My heart leapt, then fell, the confused organ having no idea how to interpret my mother's expression.

My father stepped in beside her. Another man followed, one I hadn't realized was there. At first, I was confused. Then I recognized him. Horror opened a pit in my stomach, and my soul felt like it fell out of my body.

The Monster.

I hadn't realized who he was when I was younger, but now—oh, my older self recognized this man who'd imprisoned Cass, Nix, and me.

"Who is he?" my younger self asked.

"This is a man who will help," my father said. "You haven't come into your powers because of your fear and your doubt. You are weak, but you must not be."

"You have a role to play in the great uprising," my mother said. "We depend upon you. Without you, the demons will fail. You *must* come into your powers."

"What?" My shocked gaze traveled between them. I'd known they had great plans for me, but not the extent of them. What did all this mean?

"You must go with this man now," my mother said.

My gaze darted to his face. His expression was so cold that it chilled the entire room. I stepped back. "No, I don't want to."

Run! I screamed inside my mind. I couldn't bear to watch my parents give me to this man. This monster.

"You will go." My mother's voice cracked like a whip.

No! I screamed it. Over and over and over again. The world lost its color and its texture.

"Del! Wake up, Del!" Roarke gripped my shoulders gently, shaking me.

I gasped, opening my eyes. I stood in the room, but I was no longer in the past. It was just Roarke and me. Panting, I tried to get my bearings.

"What was it?" Roarke asked. "Are you all right."

No. No, I wasn't all right.

And now I realized why I'd suddenly regained my memory at this single point in my life—it was the worst moment of my existence. The very worst moment of my life.

CHAPTER NINE

It didn't take long for the chill air to drive away my panic attack. That was in the past. I had survived it. Even though my parents had given me to the Monster. *Willingly.*

But I had come out stronger. I had Cass and Nix, who I wouldn't have had otherwise.

I'd endure anything to have them by my side.

I sucked in a shuddering breath and met Roarke's concerned gaze. I smiled, going for reassuring but probably stopping somewhere closer to *only moderately freaked out.*

"You okay?" he asked.

"Yeah. Totally. I just had a flashback. It wasn't great, but I'm fine." I glanced out the window. The sun was heading for the horizon. "We need to get a move on. There's more I need to learn, and we need to find a way to Draka."

"You'll tell me later what you remembered?"

"Yes." How I was going to tell him that I was supposed to be on the side of the demons in something called a great uprising, I had no idea. That was definitely not good news.

Roarke nodded, then stepped back.

Relieved, I followed him out of the tower, not looking back as I hurried down the stairs. Fuzzy memories of this place began to return. Flashes of a warm kitchen and a great library. I hadn't left the tower often when I was a child, but when I did, those were two of the places I would go.

When we reached the bottom of the tower, I turned toward the library. "Follow me. I have an idea."

I wanted answers, not only about the layout of the castle so we could free Draka, but about myself. I hadn't been completely magically powerless as a child—I'd been a transporter. So what had my parents meant, that I hadn't come into my powers yet? My Phantom powers? Or something else?

Something that made me the Demise?

I swallowed hard and led us down the stone-paved path toward a large building at the back of the fortress. The living area was all back here, the buildings narrow and pressed up against each other. We went into a narrow side door that led to a wider hallway.

If I was remembering correctly, the library should be just off here. Whenever I wanted answers, libraries were usually where I could find them.

All of my memories were so fuzzy, but with every step through my childhood home, they grew stronger.

I led Roarke through a wide set of double doors, into a windowless room. It was massive, at least four stories tall and built entirely of the glowing Catalight stone. The light illuminated thousands of books, untouched by the elements because the room had no windows.

Of course. This was where I'd gotten my obsession with books.

"Impressive," Roarke said.

"Yeah." Cold and unwelcoming—not like my trove back home—but impressive.

A huge fireplace hulked against the far wall. Above it hung a complex tapestry. My family tree.

I hurried closer, peering up at the intricately embroidered fabric. It was an actual tree, with the oldest names at the roots and the youngest at the twig-like branches. An intricately decorated series of letters formed the base.

The World Walkers.

"What is a World Walker?" Roarke asked.

A memory of my mother flashed in my mind. I was young, no more than six, and standing in front of her throne.

"We are the last of the World Walkers," she'd intoned. Her voice, cold as ice, echoed off the stone walls of the throne room. "We have a duty. *You* have a duty. You have the strongest, deadliest power of us all. You *must* use it for the family."

I opened my mouth to ask what that meant, but the memory faded.

"I think we are able to walk between the Underworld and Earth." At least, that was the impression I'd gotten from my mother. As for my strong, deadly power? What the hell did that mean?

I searched the tree, finding that the names grew sparser at the top. I was the last one, on a spindly branch that reached toward the sky. There was nothing else to find on this tapestry.

I turned, gaze roving over the books, searching for answers.

"What are you looking for?" Roarke asked.

"I want to know what I am. What my powers are. And if there is a way to free Draka without the demons noticing us. We can't cross that barrier. It triggers them." But the library was so big, and unlike my own trove, I didn't know where to find anything.

So I did what I always did when I wanted to find something—I called on my dragon sense.

The question of who I was got no tugs. Same for anything about my powers. That information had died with my parents or was trapped in my own mind. Or my dragon sense was just too weak.

Either way, that info was lost to me for now.

But my desperate desire to find Draka *did* give me a clue.

"This way." I hurried across the library to the large desk at the far side. It was flanked on either side by suits of armor. My gaze darted to the helmets. "Holy fates. Those have horns."

"Demon armor," Roarke said.

"Yeah. That can't be good."

The desk I sought was wide and made of gleaming wood. I wasn't sure why exactly my dragon sense had taken me here. Perhaps papers or notes?

There were a few lonely sheets resting on the desk. I reached for one. As soon as my fingertips hit the desk, memories flashed in my mind. Sitting with my father, here at this desk.

His gaze was intent upon mine. "You must remember, Delphine. In the event of an attack, there is an escape tunnel behind your mother's throne. Go there. It will lead you to the outer walls near the back gate. Then you flee."

"What about you and Mother?" I asked.

"We would go, too. It is the only way to insure our line survives. If there is an attack, we must run."

My mind snapped back into the present. I met Roarke's gaze. "There's an escape tunnel near the throne where Draka is chained."

"You remembered that?"

"Yes. My father told me once when I was a child. My dragon sense knew I wanted answers, so it led me to a place where my memory would be triggered."

"That is a very handy skill."

"Indeed. When it works." I turned toward the door. "We can go get her now. We have time left on the invisibility potion."

"It's dangerous to go without your friends. We may need backup."

"What if they can't enter?" Worry for Draka felt heavy in my stomach. "We must go. We're invisible and we have an escape route. This may be our only chance. What if they move her?"

His brows drew together, worried. "You're right. If they move her, you can't find her, can you?"

"No. I thought I could before, but I was only following her directions to get to Flora at the League of FireSouls' headquarters. Finding her here, at Snowdonia, was luck. My dragon sense only found her once we were really close." I gave him my hardest look. "I'll go without you."

"I know you will." He pointed to the door. "Let's go. Do it quickly before the potion wears off. If there's a sign of danger, we leave and come back with reinforcements. We can't let the demons capture you."

"Deal." We set off, out of the library and back onto the stone pathway that was pressed up against the exterior wall.

The sun was setting now, and the bite in the air had grown stronger. I shivered as we hurried to the back of the compound. I couldn't remember what the small gate looked like, but when I spotted the wooden door, it was obviously our target.

It didn't budge under my touch, so I turned to Roarke. "Could you?"

"Yes." He broke through it the way he broke through everything. With one solid punch.

"If you weren't so destructive, you'd make a great treasure hunter," I said.

He grinned at me. "Thanks. Somehow, I feel you'd frown on my methods."

"Indeed. Destroying sites is strictly verboten," I said primly, then turned toward the now-open doorway to the mountain outside. "Now let's get a move on."

We stepped through onto a rolling bit of mountain covered by a thick layer of snow. The wind howled like a banshee as it swept across the ridge, kicking up the snow and blowing it in my eyes.

"Shit." I searched for anything that wasn't white. "I don't see the tunnel entrance."

"No, it'd be well-hidden."

I called upon my dragon sense, praying to fate it would lead me to the tunnel. We spent nearly half an hour tromping around in the snow—leaving all manner of incriminating tracks—until we finally found the tunnel exit deep beneath the snow. I was about to pull open the small wooden door when I felt the snow change.

No, it was my ice power that felt the snow change. Heat. Coming from a few dozen yards away.

"Del!" Roarke's warning came in the nick of time.

I glanced up—to exactly where my ice power was directing me—and saw a demon's fireball flying through the air, aimed straight for my head.

I lunged just as Roarke dove for me. We plowed into the snow, escaping the fireball by a hair's breadth. The demon I popped up, loading up on my ice power, and shot a massive icicle straight at the red demon who stood next to the gate.

It plowed through his middle. Red blood sprayed on the snow as he fell.

"Damn," I wheezed. "Good eye, Roarke. That was close."

"No problem."

I reached down and touched the snow, instinct propelling me. I wanted to get rid of our tracks, so I envisioned snow falling on them, just tiny, delicate ice. It worked.

In a matter of seconds, a mini blizzard covered our tracks and the demon's body.

"Good job," Roarke said.

"Thanks. I'm trying to practice more." And not be so afraid of screwing it up. "Let's go."

Roarke pulled open the hidden wooden door, and we climbed inside. It was pitch black, so I called on my Phantom power, allowing my blue glow to illuminate the tunnel.

"Whoa," I breathed.

Like the grand entrance above, the tunnel was magnificent. It was wide and beautifully paved with decorative stone in every shade of white, black, and gray.

"Your parents were not subtle people," Roarke said.

"No." I set off down the beautiful hall, vaguely ill at the excess. And coming from a FireSoul with a whole hidden treasure trove, that was saying something.

"I don't think anyone ever used this," I murmured. "If they had managed to, I wouldn't be the last of my kind, would I?"

"No, that's true. Whatever wiped out the inhabitants of this place, it did so quickly."

"I was thinking." I stuck close by his side so I could whisper. "We've only seen two demons our whole time here. So, they're sentries or something. But most of the demons can't pass the barrier in the throne room, so does that mean they're working with demons who are on Earth?"

"Yes." Roarke's voice was grim. "And I don't like it."

"Do you think the uprising you were dealing with earlier this week had anything to do with it?"

"Hard to say." He frowned. "But yes, possibly. Whatever it is, it seems well organized."

"The worst kind of demon attack."

"Exactly."

The path began to wind upward. Suddenly, stairs loomed ahead.

"I think we're getting close," I whispered.

"Agreed."

There was a brief, silent shoving match to see who would go up first. Roarke won, of course, considering that he could pick me up and set me down behind him.

He could even pick me up when I was in my Phantom form, which was annoying as heck.

I hurried up the stairs behind him. As expected, there was a flat trap door at the top, leading up to the spot by my mother's throne, I guessed.

"Do you sense anything?" Roarke's whisper was as quiet as a breeze.

There was no ice here, so I couldn't feel for the warmth of bodies. But I couldn't hear anything, so I shook my head.

"Then we'll go." He pressed his big palms flat to the trap door.

I grabbed his arm, the transparent blue of my Phantom form stark against his black jacket. "Wait! Let me check. I'll just stick my head through."

"Just your head. If you see anything, we run. You first."

"Fine." I joined him on the top stair and slowly stuck my head through the floor. It was so weird, almost funny. Like I was a cartoon.

As soon as my eyes cleared the door, I saw Draka, still chained in her human form and lying on the ground. Did she look skinnier? Were they feeding her?

Besides Draka, the room was empty.

Good.

I popped up through the floor, not bothering to tell Roarke. He'd figure it out. I raced to Draka, keeping my gaze on the room around me. Roarke was so fast, he was at my side as I fell to my knees in front of her. Her features were as timeless as ever.

"Draka! Wake up!" As I spoke, a massive silver cage fell down around us, clattering on the stone floor. It was huge and square, trapping us.

Panic clenched my heart.

"Damn it." Roarke's deep voice echoed in the stone chamber.

Draka's eyes flared wide as she looked around blindly. "Who's there?"

"It's me, Del. I'm invisible." I reached for her hands, and she clutched at them, turning toward me.

Roarke knelt at the cage side and tried to lift it, but it wouldn't budge. Magic. He was more than strong enough to lift the thing. Trying not to lose my shit, I left him to get us out of the cage while I turned back to Draka.

"I've got to get you out of those chains. Help me!" I pulled at the heavy metal shackles around her transparent blue wrists, searching for a lock of some kind. How had they found something that could hold a Phantom?

"You can't. It's impossible. As long as I'm trapped in human form, I can't escape these. You cannot release me." Grief crossed her features. "And you weren't supposed to come for me! Flora was supposed to stop you."

"That's why you sent me to her."

"Yes! The demons were forcing me to make a connection with you to draw you here. It was the only way to make them think I did what they commanded. I sent you a message, but they didn't know what kind."

"A message to keep me from coming for you? Nothing would keep me from rescuing a friend."

"I'm not your friend." She tried to harden her face, but I could see what she was doing. I'd felt her love in my dreams. "Go now!"

Behind her, Roarke had shifted and was trying to punch through the cage's enchantment. It wasn't working.

"I can't leave you." I tugged at the chains, fear and frustration rising in my chest. Any moment, demons would come. "How the hell did they manage to trap a Phantom dragon?"

"They've taken my source egg." Devastation hovered in her gaze. "As long as it is trapped, I cannot shift to escape."

"Where is it?"

"Their stronghold. It is too well-guarded—it will never be freed. Leave me." She gripped my hands, desperation in her grip. "You *must* run! Don't let them catch you. You are the Guardian, not the Demise. But if they catch you…"

I hated to point out that they already had. "Tell me where it is!"

"No!" Her expression was hard as granite. "You would never survive. It's too heavily guarded. You don't know what they are capable of."

"Del," Roarke whispered. "We've got company. And I can't get us out."

Shit.

Demons came from the far doors, not from the walls like last time. They must not have expected us back so soon and hadn't been lying in wait, but we'd triggered their trap all the same.

"You're invisible. When they lift the cage, you must slip away and run," Draka said. "Do not come back for me. It is what they want. I am a trap. For *you*."

My heart tore in two—she was in this because of me.

More demons poured from the door. Two dozen. No, three. Four.

We couldn't fight four dozen demons. They surrounded the cage, so many species. All of their gazes searched the space inside. Their noses twitched.

"Where are they?" one grumbled. "I smell them but don't see them."

"They're somewhere," another said.

"Does the air look funny in there?" A demon pointed into the cage.

Shit. Was the potion wearing off?

"Could be a spell," a gray demon said. "Surround the cage. Then lift it."

They formed a barrier around the edges, leaving no spot for us to escape.

Roarke turned to me and mouthed, *Distraction*.

An idea popped into my mind.

As a demon with glowing hands lifted up the cage, I called on my power over the past, letting it flow through me. I pulled it forward, trying to bring back a point where this room would have been flooded with people.

My mother's fortieth birthday. It'd been a huge party—one I had heard from my tower. The suit of demon armor in the library showed how chummy my parents had been with demons. What would they think of this lot appearing at the party?

Like a barreling freight train, the past came hurtling back. The room filled with revelers, over a thousand of them. They danced and drank and sang, all dressed in crazy costumes in a rainbow of colors. A five-piece band played in the corner, filling the stone room with raucous music.

Roarke darted toward the edge of the cage, slipping a hand under the bottom edge just before the partiers noticed the four dozen demons in their midst. Screams sounded. Immediately, the partiers and the demons collided in a fight.

When a mage attacked two of the demons near the cage, a hole opened up that we could run through.

"Come on," Roarke whispered.

"Hurry!" Draka hissed. "Your invisibility charm is fading!"

I gave her one last look, then ran to Roarke and slipped out from beneath the cage.

"Don't come back!" Draka called.

Roarke followed me out. The demons were all busy fighting the party guests, most of whom were powerful supernaturals. There were shifters, mages, sorceresses, and fae, among others. Magic flew through the air as destructive spells were cast.

"To the main exit," I said. There were more people between us and the trap door, so we sprinted the other way, dodging and weaving between bodies.

Out of the corner of my eye, I thought I caught a glimpse of my mother. Torn, I looked away and pushed myself faster toward the door. We just had to make it to the midpoint of the room—where the demons couldn't pass.

We were almost there when something heavy slammed into my back. I stumbled, losing my footing. I slammed to the ground, barely catching myself with my hands.

Roarke crashed down behind me. I struggled to rise, but a heavy iron chain held me tight to the ground.

A woman kicked me in the stomach. Pain flared and I curled in on myself.

We were no longer invisible.

And we were caught.

Someone kicked me in the head, and I blacked out.

CHAPTER TEN

I surfaced from the blackness slowly. Pain was the first thing I noticed. My head ached, and my stomach felt like someone had set a bowling ball on it.

Groggily, I blinked, slowly taking in the fact that I was slung over the shoulder of some massive demon. My wrists were bound with thick metal shackles. I tried to struggle, but my limbs were so heavy they could have been made of iron. Worse, my mind felt like it was running at half speed.

A sedative?

It was all I could do to keep my eyes open, so I assumed yes.

I tilted my head to the left, catching a glimpse of Roarke. It took three demons to carry his unconscious body. We had a guard of at least twelve, all massive demons of a variety of species.

My heart thundered. Where the hell were they taking us?

All around us, massive trees reached up into the sky. Not as big as redwoods, but close. A hazy black mist snaked around the tree trunks, bringing with it the most visceral sensation of evil.

My stomach lurched. I swallowed hard.

If I could just shift, maybe…

I gave it my all, calling upon my Phantom magic, but something stopped it.

The shackles.

Damn it—they were the magic-dampening kind.

"Quit your wriggling." The demon who held me gave me a hard shake.

I was about to punch him in the back when a big hand shoved a smelly rag in front of my mouth and nose. I thrashed, trying to break free, but my mind began to shut down, wooziness pulling at me.

"Told you we didn't give her enough of the stuff," a gruff voice muttered.

It was the last thing I heard before I blacked out entirely.

I snapped awake.

Darkness.

Everything was darkness. The stone floor was cold and damp. The dungeon silent. No noise, not even the soft breathing of my only companions.

Where were my friends? Had the Monster taken them? My heart jumped into my throat as I scrambled upright.

"Cass? Nix?"

No answer.

Tears sprang to my eyes as my chest clenched in panic. I crawled from my spot, blindly seeking them. After a few feet, a chain tugged at my wrist, cutting into my skin.

I was chained? I wasn't normally chained in the dungeon.

Memories slammed into my mind, stealing my breath.

I wasn't in the Monster's dungeon. And he hadn't taken my friends.

Because I wasn't fifteen anymore.

Relief made my muscles turn to water. *Anything* was better than being in the Monster's dungeon. I sagged against the ground. I reached up to touch my lucky necklace and felt the heavy weight of iron around my wrists.

I licked my lips, tasting the sweet remnants of whatever chemical the demons had used to knock me unconscious.

I sucked in a ragged breath and tried to take stock of my surroundings. The demons had taken me somewhere and chained me up, alone in a dark dungeon. Now that my eyes had adjusted, I saw the sliver of light beneath the door. It was dim, but gave just enough brightness to reveal that I was alone.

Where was Roarke? Dark magic was strong on the air, bringing with it the scent of a garbage fire. It was pure evil. Where the hell was I?

My skin prickled with nerves.

Nowhere I wanted to stay, that was for damned sure.

I reached up for my comms charm, but it was gone. Lost or taken, I didn't know which. But I was definitely alone.

I called upon my Phantom form, praying to fate that it worked.

Nothing happened.

"Damn it!" I shook my wrists, tugging at the magical chains that dampened my magic. They were stuck hard into the wall.

Freaking things!

Roarke was probably trapped, too. Draka needed me. And inside this dungeon, there was every chance my location was shielded from my *deirfiúr*. I needed to get the hell out of here or Draka would die in those chains, tied up near my mother's throne.

Which somehow made it even grosser, though I couldn't quite pinpoint why.

A voice sounded from outside. I stilled, listening.

A demon was somewhere at the other end of the hall. My heart raced. Was he coming for me?

Then I heard a key scratch in the cell door's lock.

I reached out, trying to get a feel for the magical signature of whoever was entering. Heat warmed my skin, and the smell of iron hit my nose.

A gift over metal, maybe?

I could use that.

Quietly, I lay down, pretending to be unconscious. For good measure, I pulled my shirt up, revealing my stomach. It made me gag, but I tried to pose sexily. Unconscious girls weren't sexy unless you were a pervy criminal, but if I had to bet these demons were probably pervy criminals.

And I wanted this one to get close.

The key *snicked* in the lock, and the door creaked open.

I shoved aside the desperate desire to open my eyes and lay still. I could just make out the demon's footsteps as he approached.

A big foot nudged me in the side, and the demon said, "Wake up. The Masters want to have some fun with you."

The dark glee in his voice made sweat break out on my skin. I could feel his gaze crawling over me like roaches. I snapped my eyes open and lunged for the figure towering over me.

I slammed into his legs, taking him to the ground, and pinned him. He thrashed beneath me and would have thrown me off if I hadn't managed to grab a handful of his balls.

Bile rose in my throat as I squeezed. But the demon stilled, so...jackpot.

"I bet you like these, huh?" I said.

He grunted.

"You know, I could tear these right off." I squeezed. "In fact, it's how I like to spend a Saturday night. I don't even like to use knives. Just...*yank*."

I pulled for good measure, and he made a weird wheezing noise.

Fates. I was so glad I didn't have a pair of these liabilities.

"You got a key to these chains?" I asked.

He shook his head frantically.

"No problem," I said. "Because I think you have a metal gift. You can melt it, can't you?"

I held my breath, praying I'd guessed right by the smell of his magic.

He didn't say anything, so I squeezed again.

He gasped. "Yes!"

"Then melt these chains off me," I demanded. My stomach lurched as I said it because this was going to hurt a hell of a lot.

"Crazy bitch," he muttered.

"Yeah, you're probably right." I could've had him melt the chain links, but if I still wore the cuffs, my magic would be dampened. And if I wanted to get Roarke out of here, too, I'd need my magic. "Do it anyway."

"No!"

"Fine." I squeezed hard and started to pull, fully intending to live up to my promise but knowing I'd probably puke if I had to do it.

Yeah, one hundred percent, I'd vomit if this demon made me deliver on my gruesome promise.

The demon stiffened, then whined, "Fine, fine!"

I kept my grip on my prize and held up one wrist in front of his face. "Do it fast, or you'll regret it."

He grimaced, his rough features twisting, and touched his fingertip to my cuff. In a flash, it turned molten red and dripped off my wrist. For a moment, it hurt like hell, making my stomach turn, then nothing. But I could smell my burned flesh. Probably singed all the nerves right off.

I switched hands, trying not to brush my charred skin against his clothes, and demanded, "The other one."

He nodded sharply and repeated the drill.

This time, I was ready for the pain, but it didn't make it any easier. I bit my tongue, which, no surprise, didn't help. But as soon as the metal melted off my wrist, I called my sword from the ether. I gripped the blade tight, holding it to the demon's throat.

"But, but... I-I freed you," he stuttered.

"I haven't torn off your balls, have I? So I've kept my end of the deal." I pressed the metal into his neck until a thin line of blood appeared. "Where are they keeping the other prisoner? The man they abducted with me."

His eyes widened. "I don't know. Really!"

I pressed the blade harder, but he stuttered the same thing.

"Fine." I sliced his throat with the blade, deep and sure.

The surprise and betrayal in his eyes just before their light faded sent the tiniest twinge of guilt through me, but I needed his power if I wanted to free Roarke.

And he *was* a demon who'd been so gleeful at the idea of the Masters having *fun* with me.

So, yeah. I slit his throat.

And as he was bleeding out, I called upon my Phantom magic, turning blue and transparent, then I pulled the soul out of his body. Without a qualm, I stole his power over metal. The wispy white soul came straight to me, and I absorbed his gift, smelling the hot iron and feeling the warmth against my skin.

When I was done, I hopped up, leaving his body without a second glance.

The time for hesitation was over. There may have been risk in stealing powers, and I may have had a difficult time controlling them, but I had to fight if we were going to win. And to fight, I needed magic.

CHAPTER ELEVEN

I hesitated at the cell door, peering around the edge and into the hall. As I'd thought, it was dimly lit by a single forty-watt bulb hanging from a chain.

Honestly, I was surprised it had electricity, considering how old everything else was. The floor and walls were made of the same rough stone that my cell had been, and all of it was ancient looking.

I sucked in a deep breath and called on my dragon sense, asking it to help me find Roarke. It picked up the trail right away, leading me left down the hall. I passed several more cell doors, but they were cracked open slightly.

We were the only prisoners, thank magic. I didn't want to have to waste time and energy saving someone else, though I wouldn't have been capable of abandoning them here.

Roarke wasn't on this floor, I realized. He was lower down. I followed my dragon sense down a narrow set of stairs, gagging slightly at the smell of blood and misery. When I reached the bottom, there was a wooden door.

I pushed on it, but it stuck. Locked.

A smile tugged at my lips as I touched the metal lock. I reached for the magic I'd stolen, letting its warmth flow through me and into the metal. The lock glowed bright orange, then melted down the wood and puddled on the ground.

Before it could cool and form a doorstopper, I pushed open the door.

Shock stole my breath.

It was a torture chamber. A full-on, creepy, horror movie nightmare of chains and whips and weird stuff I didn't even recognize. A large man was strung up by his hands, bruises covering his bare torso. The two demons who stood in front of him turned to face me, their lips curled up in annoyance.

Dread curled in my stomach as I got a better look at the victim.

Roarke.

Rage unlike any I'd ever known blossomed in my chest like a flower made of acid.

"Bastards!"

Before they could speak, I charged up a massive icicle and sent it through the stomach of the gray demon on the left. Blood sprayed as he fell backwards. The other demon drew a sword, but before he could strike, I hit him with an icicle. Right through the stomach again.

I wanted them to die slowly.

I considered cutting out their tongues so they couldn't tell anyone I'd saved Roarke, but I didn't have the stomach for that kind of torture. And anyway, it'd be pretty obvious who'd busted him out of here.

While the demons writhed on the ground, I raced for Roarke.

"Roarke!" He hung limply by his wrists, his chest a mess of bruises.

I dipped low to look up into his face, then patted his cheek gently. "Come on, guy. You gotta wake up. We're making a run for it."

My heart split in two as his eyes opened slowly. It just lay there in my chest like a broken coffee cup.

"Del?" Confusion laced his voice.

"Yeah. Can you stand?"

He shook his head as if to clear it, then put his weight on his legs. He winced, then nodded. "Yeah. I'm good. Let's get out of here."

His voice was rough, and I didn't want to think of why. I glanced at the shackles on his wrist. There were keyholes in them. Unlocking them would be better than burning him if I had to melt them off. My wrists still hurt like hell, and he'd been beaten enough.

"Hang on," I said. "I'm gonna see if one of these jerks has a key."

He nodded and I hurried to the body of the demon nearest me.

I was only a few feet from Roarke when I heard the chains rattle. I glanced back to see that his legs had given out again. I almost puked, right there in the torture chamber. Just the idea of what had been done to him made me want to be ill. This whole place made me want to be ill.

If I could get out of here without losing my lunch, it'd be a miracle.

But Roarke's injuries... Fear chilled me. I had no idea how I'd drag a guy as big as him out of here if he couldn't walk on his own.

I'd freaking figure it out, though.

I knelt at the body of the demon at my feet. He was panting raggedly as he bled out. I didn't spare him a glance as I patted him down. My need for vengeance had been smothered by my concern for Roarke. It was still there, burning low, but I didn't have time to waste on something so petty. I had one goal, and that was to get us the hell out of here.

The demon had nothing on him except a wicked looking knife, so I moved on to the next one. This one was nearly dead, his red face ashen and nearly gray. He also had no keys.

"Damn it," I muttered. I glanced up, searching for a key ring. Like this was some well-organized home on Pinterest, or something.

I didn't spot any keyring hooks, but I did see a shelf cluttered with vials of potion. Acids and poisons?

A memory flashed in my mind, of Nix telling me about some twisted torturers from the Underworld who would beat up their victims, then give them a healing potion so they could just beat them up again.

"Oh, please, fate," I whispered as I called on my dragon sense. I begged it to find me a healing potion, feeding it my desperate desire to heal Roarke.

My dragon sense tugged right away, pulling me toward the potions. Unerringly, I reached for a silver vial on the right. My burned wrists twinged with pain as I picked it up. I pulled the cork and sniffed the potion.

Didn't smell evil. Kinda sweet.

I uncorked it and knocked on my head, then licked a drop off the stopper. Waited a second. I didn't die, so I considered it a win. And my wrists felt a bit better, though they were still charred to a crisp. I forced myself to look at them. The edges of the burn looked a bit better.

Confident that I'd found a healing potion, I hurried back to Roarke. I lifted his head and said, "Wake up. We've got to get out of here."

He opened his eyes, and his gaze met mine. The misery cleared from his face as he looked at me.

"I'm going to get you out of these chains, okay? Then you're going to drink a potion to heal you."

He nodded, his gaze slightly cloudy. I wrapped my arms around his waist and pulled his body away from his left arm. I'd do that one first, and I didn't want the molten metal dripping on him.

"You've got to try to stand, okay?" Sweat dotted my skin as I tried to hold his two-hundred pound body away from his cuffed wrist and reached up to touch the shackle. I forced my new magic into it as quickly as I could. In a flash, it turned orange and melted off.

Roarke barely flinched, though I smelled his burning flesh.

I kept an eye on the molten metal at my feet and shifted Roarke the other way, hoping he would stay upright. I melted the other shackle. This time, he jerked.

Once the chain no longer held him up, he stumbled backward. I tried to keep him upright, but he was too big.

We both fell in a pile, but he righted himself on his own, sitting up. I knelt by his side.

"Magic's sake, I'm weak as a kitten," he muttered.

"You're one big bruise and you have multiple broken bones. Who knows what else." Honestly, I didn't want to know. I held the vial up to his lips. "Drink this."

He drank it, grimacing as he swallowed.

I held my breath as I watched him, praying that the potion would work. Color returned to his cheeks, and his gaze brightened. The worst of the gruesome bruises on his chest faded, and the skin on his wrists healed. He still looked like hell—not everything had been cured, but he looked much more...alive.

"It worked!" I grinned. "Now let's get the hell out of here. Can you stand?"

"Yes." He squeezed my shoulder. "Thanks for saving me. You're a badass."

"I know." I reached down to help him stand.

He took my hand. Though he was improved, he wasn't close to full strength. But he was steady on his own two feet, for which I couldn't thank fate enough.

"You good?" I asked.

"Yes. Hang on." Roarke headed to the back of the room and picked up a shirt and jacket that had been tossed on the ground.

As he tugged them on, I called on my dragon sense. Where was Draka's egg? Could it be here? Was this the fortress she'd talked about? If the demons were going to catch me, perhaps they would take me to their headquarters.

For a while, my dragon sense picked up nothing. I fed it my desire to save Draka, envisioning the other dragon source eggs that I'd seen at the quarry cave last week.

Please, please, please.

This had to work.

Finally, it tugged. Just slightly, so faint that I might not have noticed it. Lately, my dragon sense had seemed to be getting stronger, and I was grateful.

"Draka's source egg is somewhere in this castle," I said.

"Close?"

"Um, no. It's either fairly far or well-guarded from me. By magic, possibly."

"Then we need backup."

"Yeah." We did. Trying to save Draka alone hadn't gone well. I wouldn't get too many second chances, so I wasn't going to risk it. "Let's get out of here. Recoup. Make a plan."

Roarke nodded. The gray mist of his magic formed a small tornado around him as he shifted into his demon form. "Pays to be prepared."

"Couldn't agree more."

We hurried from the room, our steps silent. I let my dragon sense lead me out of the dungeons, following it up the narrow stone steps and onto the main hallway. We passed all the doors and reached the heavy wooden one at the end. A push revealed that it was locked.

This had to be the main entrance to the dungeons. Would there be a guard on the other side?

"When we go in, I'll take left and you take right, okay?" I said.

"Perfect."

I kept my sword ready as I touched the metal lock. It melted in a flash, and I pushed the door open. Shuffling sounded from inside.

I rushed in, veering left. Roarke went right.

On my side, a guard had just stood up from his chair. He was a hulking red demon with short horns and a leather vest. Fire demon, probably. When he raised a hand that glowed red, it confirmed it.

Instead of firing an icicle at him, which was becoming old hat at this point, I shot some nearly frozen water from my hand. Slush, basically. When it splatted on his raised hand, I used my magic to freeze it.

An icy mitt formed on his hand that suppressed his fire throwing ability.

Sweet!

He growled and raised his other hand, throwing a fireball before I could freeze him. I turned corporeal and deflected it with my blade, then lunged, sinking the blade into his chest.

I pulled the sword free. He tottered, shock spread across his face.

"Weren't expecting me?" I grinned and planted a boot in his midsection, toppling him over.

I turned to Roarke just as he tore the head off the other guard and tossed it on the ground. Blood splattered his chest.

"Got some pent-up aggression?" I asked.

"You don't even know."

I grinned, then turned and headed for the door. We crept through the winding halls of the fortress, following my dragon sense. I asked it to find me the quietest, least guarded exit and prayed that it would work. It didn't always—just like when I'd asked it to find me Draka at my old home. It had taken me to Draka, but I'd forgotten to cover all my bases and hadn't asked it not to take me across a threshold to the Underworld.

We climbed a wide set of stairs to the next level, reaching a heavy wooden door at the top. It wasn't locked, so Roarke pushed it open slowly while I peeked around the edge. The hall was wide and empty.

We hurried through the door and toward the exit. Rooms dotted the hall here and there, but they were all empty as we passed.

At the end of the hall, the wide wooden door cracked open.

Someone was coming!

I lunged into the nearest open door. Roarke followed. We pressed ourselves against the wall, breath held.

Footsteps neared. At least five pairs.

My heart leapt into my throat. When I noticed the mirror on the wall across from me, my head swam. If the people in the hall glanced in, they might see our reflection!

I gripped my sword and stared hard at the mirror, praying to fate as they passed. Roarke was ready, his stance that of a warrior prepared to fight.

The figures passed by a moment later. Five demons. One started to turn, but his companion said something and he didn't.

When a door clicked shut farther down the hallway, my muscles relaxed a fraction. We gave them a few minutes, then peeked out.

Coast was clear.

We crept out and hurried to the door. Fortunately, it was near an exterior wall. And it was nighttime. A sliver of moon hung in the sky, visible just over the high walls of the fortress. The air was chilly, but nothing like my family's place in Wales.

We were at a back entrance to the castle, if I had to guess. The doors were all small and the architecture not very ornate. Perfect for servants and the working class. A wild courtyard stretched in front of us. Not manicured like many courtyards, but rather a little patch of the forest right inside the castle walls. A river ran through it, fresh water for the fortress in times of siege.

My dragon sense pulled me toward the river. I followed it, hurrying across the open courtyard and darting for the shadow of the main wall.

"That's your exit, isn't it?" Roarke pointed to the metal grate where the river flowed out through the castle wall.

My dragon sense screamed, *Yes!*

"Yep," I said. "I asked for the most hidden exit. We got it."

But the massive iron grate blocked our exit. The gaps were wide enough for water and even small fish, but they were built to keep people out.

"Just watch my back." I jumped into the river, grateful that it was only as deep as my waist and fairly sluggish. The water was chilly, making goosebumps pop up on my skin. I waded toward the grate, reaching out with one finger and pressing it to the iron.

I called upon my new magic, feeding it into the gate. At first, nothing happened. It was a lot of metal. I dug deep, calling upon more magic. My head grew light as I focused on melting the metal. There was just so much of it!

Finally, the metal began to glow red. Just a small section, but it spread. I pushed myself, feeding it more and more of my power. Slowly, the metal poured downward, warming the water around me.

A scuffle sounded from behind. I turned, catching sight of Roarke breaking the neck of a demon guard.

"Hurry," he said. "More may come."

I turned back to the grate, feeding it more magic. Finally, I had a hole big enough for the two of us to escape. I didn't dare try for more. I was already close to running out of power. I didn't have an infinite well, like Cass. I was nearly tapped out and would need to recuperate.

"Come on." I climbed through the gap in the metal grate.

Roarke followed, dragging the body with him. Once he'd climbed through the hole, he pulled out the body and let it float downstream. I pressed my hand to the metal of the ruined grate and envisioned the metal melting and rebuilding itself.

I was panting by the time the metal began to glow and flow upward, forcing as much of my magic into it as I could manage. But we really needed to cover our tracks. The orange metal rebuilt itself, reforming the grate. If you looked closely, it was a poorly done job. I needed more practice. But hopefully the demons wouldn't notice and have an easier time tracking us.

"Come on," Roarke said.

"Okay." I removed my hand, weak from spending all my magic.

We waded down the river until we could find a place to climb out. Massive trees surrounded us. We were in the same large, dark forest where I'd woken from my stupor while being carried by the demon.

Out here, the air felt fresher. Like it wasn't heavy with the evil that pervaded the fortress we'd just escaped from. But I remembered waking up while being carried through here initially. It'd felt evil then. Just went to show how relative things could be. This forest was still full of dark magic—just less than the creepy place we'd escaped.

"We need to find somewhere to recover," I said. "I'm drained, and I lost my comms charm so I can't call Cass to come get us."

"I could use a break, too." He looked around, taking in the tall trees and the tainted black mist that hung low on the ground. "If we could only find a graveyard or haunted place, I could make an Underpath."

"Are you really up to it?" He still looked so beat up.

"You're right. I may need to rest. Let's try to find some place sheltered."

We raced through the forest, trying to cover as much ground as possible but still keep the fortress in our sights. It went out of view occasionally, but I always knew where it was. I didn't want to lose it now that we'd found it.

Night animals rustled as we ran, shrieks and howls making my hair stand on end. My legs were freezing from the water by the time we'd gone a couple miles, and I was desperate to find a place to hole up.

When we came upon a wide waterfall that fed a river, I pulled up short. It was about twenty feet tall and ten feet wide, a thick fall of water that pounded down on the rocks below. Dim moonlight glinted on the water.

"Is there a cave behind that waterfall?" I asked. There was a dark patch at the side.

"Possibly."

"Let's check it out." I clambered over the rocks at the side of the waterfall, finding a gap between the water and the stone. I squeezed inside, finding a passageway. "Jackpot."

Roarke followed me in, and we hurried down the passage, coming out in a cave the size of a small house. It even had a bit of rustic furniture.

"Does someone live here?" Roarke asked.

I explored, finding a hearth in the middle of the room, along with a couch, bed, and rustic kitchen. It'd all been handmade of wood, possibly from the forest, and looked like it'd been abandoned for years.

"I think whoever lived here has left," I said.

"Didn't like their neighbors."

"Wouldn't surprise me." I glanced around. "This is a little too good to be true. I don't know if we should stay here. We could be trapped."

Roarke pointed to the back of the room. "I think that's another exit."

He went to it and disappeared. I followed. This path was narrower than the one we'd entered through, but it eventually spit us out into the forest.

"Two entrances. That's good," Roarke said.

"Yeah." I shivered, my whole body now freezing, not just my legs. "If only we had some guard dogs to warn us if people were coming."

"You're friends with plenty of magical dogs," Roarke said. "And I don't think we can go much farther until you warm up and get your strength back."

"Look that bad, do I?" My chattering teeth really punctuated the question.

"Just tired."

"Yeah." But he was right. I did have plenty of magical canine friends and just about no energy left. I called Pond Flower with my mind, praying she'd show up. There was nothing for a while, but finally, she appeared in front of me.

"Pond Flower!" I knelt and rubbed her ears. She gave me a sloppy kiss on the cheek. "Can you be our guard dog? Maybe get one of your friends to guard the other exit?"

She nodded and was about to disappear when I reached out a hand. "Hang on. Could you also tell Corin we're here? And get some food from the kitchen at the FireSoul compound?"

My stomach growled as Pond Flower cocked her head. I could only hope she understood or could do either of those things.

"That's a pretty handy talent," Roarke said.

I shrugged. "Just lucky to have good friends, I guess."

It took a few minutes, but Pond Flower returned with the black hellhound we'd met outside the FireSouls' compound. Pond Flower had a big hunk of ham in her mouth, but no Corin. The big black hound had a loaf of crusty bread.

"One out of two ain't bad," I said. "And it was too much to hope she could transport Corin."

Roarke reached for the hunk of ham, scratching Pond Flower's ears when she gave it up easily. "You're one of a kind, you know?"

Pond Flower's tongue lolled out of her mouth.

I took the bread from the black dog and said, "Thank you for coming."

I wished I knew its name, but Emile, the only true Anima Mage that I knew, would have to ask the dog for me.

The black dog nodded and set up guard at this exit. Pond Flower followed us back into the homey space, then headed toward the waterfall.

"I'll start a fire," Roarke said. He set to work at the small hearth, making use of the dry kindling and wood. He picked up a couple of little rocks and struck them together.

"You can make fire from rocks?" I asked.

"I don't know. I hope so."

I grinned, then set off to shake the dust from the blankets. I piled them on the couch by the fire, then scavenged a bucket from the rustic kitchen. It only took a moment to get water from the waterfall out front. I gave Pond Flower a scratch, then returned to the little room.

By the time I returned, Roarke had built the fire. He wore a blanket wrapped around his waist like a long towel, and his wet clothes were laid out by the fire to dry. The firelight flickered off his muscles, and my gaze roved over his chest.

"Genius plan." My own wet clothes were cold and stiff. I set the bucket by the couch. "Turn around. I'm going to do the same."

Roarke grinned, then turned. Quickly, I stripped out of my clothes and laid them out, then draped a blanket over my shoulders. My toes were like little bricks of ice, but the rest of me was starting to warm up.

I hurried to the couch, which was built of wood and upholstered in some kind of rough fabric. I curled up on the cushion, tucking my feet under me. The couch was stuffed with something lumpy, but it was mostly soft. I was beyond grateful for the bounty of this little abandoned cave.

Roarke was still turned around, so I said, "You can come join me."

"Excellent." He went to the table in the kitchen, retrieved the bread and ham the dogs had brought us, and took a seat next to me.

I piled some of the blankets on top of us and leaned into his heat. Immediately, exhaustion pulled at me, as if my body had been waiting for a single moment of relaxation. Then it struck.

I yawned hard. "I'm glad you're here with me."

"Me, too." Roarke offered me the bread and ham.

I took the bread and bit in, not even caring about the fact that it had hellhound spit on it. We chowed down, so hungry that we didn't take time to talk. When the food was polished off, we drank from the bucket.

I handed the thing off to Roarke and wiped my mouth, then collapsed back on the couch. We had so much to talk about, but my eyelids were so heavy.

Roarke sat back, and I curled up against him. His warmth soaked into me, the best thing I'd ever felt. I tried to open my mouth to ask one of my million questions. But nothing came out except a yawn. Roarke's eyes were at half-mast, too.

His gaze dropped to my wrists. Concern wrinkled his brow.

"Your wrists. They're burned, too," he said. "You didn't heal yourself with the potion."

"I'm fine." Though they hurt like hell. "I tasted the potion to make sure it wasn't poison. It healed them a bit."

"You should have healed yourself first."

"When have you ever healed yourself before me?" I tried to stifle my yawn, but failed.

"Del." Something heavy laced his voice, but I couldn't identify it.

"Del, what?"

He didn't have an answer. I glanced up, my eyelids feeling like they weighed a million pounds. His eyes were closed, his breathing steady. The torture had taken its toll. Not to mention everything we'd gone through before and after.

I couldn't keep my eyes open anymore and didn't bother trying. The fire warmed me, we were safe— mostly—and I'd had a decent meal. There was no point in fighting sleep. Not when it was going to take me anyway.

But as I drifted off, I couldn't help but think how good it felt to trust Roarke. Having him by my side felt right. And I felt lucky.

CHAPTER TWELVE

When I woke, the fire had died. I was still curled up against Roarke, my muscles stiff, but I felt much stronger, so it was a win.

I had a desperate urge to pee, so I made my way to the back exit, finding the black hellhound still loyally guarding. The sun was rising over the dark trees. Though it should have made the forest feel more cheerful, it didn't. Nothing could improve this place as long as the stink of evil hovered over it.

"Good morning." I scratched the dog's ears, then found a bush to use.

By the time I returned to the main room, Roarke was awake, dressed in his pants and boots, and pulling on his shirt.

"Feeling better?" I asked.

"Much." His voice was strong, no longer exhausted or pained. "You?"

"Yeah. Turn around."

He did, and I changed quickly into my dry clothes. They were stiff and dirty, but I couldn't complain. I tugged on my shirt last, then said, "Okay, I'm good."

Roarke turned and took a seat on the couch. "Come sit. We need to make a plan."

I joined him, curling up at his side and absorbing his warmth. My mind immediately turned toward the fortress. "So, where the hell are we? Earth or the Underworld?"

"Earth," Roarke said. "I'd feel it if this were the Underworld. But where on Earth, I have no idea."

"It's creepy. And I bet whoever lives in that damned fortress is even creepier."

"They're demons, though possibly not all of them. And they have contacts with demons in the Underworld, I think."

"Not good."

"No." He frowned. "Whatever this is has been growing under my watch. It's my responsibility."

"And mine, if I'm the Guardian."

He scrubbed a hand over his hair. "They think you're something important, that's for sure. They were questioning me about you."

My stomach lurched. "That's why they were torturing you?"

"Yes. Those cuffs knocked out my powers, and they dosed me with something strong for good measure. I don't think they realized who I am or I'd be dead. They just knew that I was with you."

"Did you learn anything from them?"

"No. They were asking all the questions. What do you think they want with you?"

I swallowed hard, not wanting to share what I'd remembered at my parents' house.

But I'd decided to trust him, hadn't I?

I took a deep breath and stepped off the cliff. "When we were at my parents' place"—I couldn't think of it as my own home—"I remembered a conversation with my parents. I'm supposed to be on the side of the demons in something called the great uprising."

His arm tightened on my shoulders, then relaxed. "That's why you're called the Demise."

"I would think so, yes." I drew in a shuddery breath. "And I'm supposed to have a stronger, deadlier power than my parents. But I have no idea what it is. Maybe that's one reason I've been so hesitant to take powers. My subconscious knows I'm supposed to do something bad."

"You'll only do something bad if you choose to. And I know you won't."

"I hope you're right." I squeezed his hand, but worry still clouded my mind. "Right now, we have one important goal. Save Draka."

"We need to get out of here and get some backup."

"Yeah. We can't do this on our—"

A rustling noise sounded from the passageway on the waterfall side. I sat up.

Then footsteps. We leapt to our feet. My heart climbed into my throat as I prayed that something terrible hadn't happened to Pond Flower. I called on my gift over ice, readying an icicle.

Shadowy forms appeared at the passage entrance a moment later. I was about to hurl my icy spear when I realized it was Cass. And Nix and Aidan. Pond Flower padded behind them.

"Guys!" I stowed the icicle. "How did you find us?"

"When you didn't show up after a while, we used our dragon sense to find you." Nix strolled toward me. "Took a little while, though. This place is remote."

"Where are we?" I asked.

"Central Germany. In the mountains," Aidan said.

My *deirfiúr* reached me, and I hugged them. "Thank you so much for coming."

"Of course," Nix said.

"So, what's the deal? Why are you hiding out in a cave?" Cass asked.

I explained our abduction and the fortress and Draka's egg. Their expressions grew more dire the longer I talked.

"So now we need to break in and steal the egg," Nix said.

"Exactly," I said. "But we need some supplies first. Cass, could you transport back to Magic's Bend and bring back invisibility potions from Connor, food, and some fresh clothes? Oh, and a truth serum, if he has one."

"Truth serum?" Cass asked.

"Yeah. Maybe I'll get lucky and meet someone to interrogate. I want to know more about their plans."

"Any idea who?" Aidan asked.

"I wish. But at this point, it pays to be prepared."

Roarke reached for my hand and squeezed it.

"Yeah, agreed," Cass said. "I'll be back in a jiffy. Then we can talk about how we're breaking into this fortress."

The sun was high in the sky by the time we departed the cave, though it was still cold as the abominable snowman's butt. Aidan had used his healing ability to take care of the worst of my wrist burns, and Cass had returned with everything I'd asked for. After changing and eating, I'd been ready to take on the world.

Which was good, because I didn't have much choice.

Each of us had an invisibility potion in our pocket. We wanted them to last as long as possible, so we'd drink them as soon as we got through the castle walls.

As we crept through the forest, black mist twined around the tree trunks like a sentient being, bringing misery with it wherever it touched.

"This place is so creepy," Nix murmured.

"Yeah," I said. "Can't get out of here soon enough."

"I think it's coming from the fortress," Roarke said. "Feels similar to the way it did in there."

He was right. The memory of the evil stink of the fortress made me shudder.

The fortress wall appeared through the trees a moment later. I stopped my friends and turned to them. "You guys wait here. I'm going to see if I can melt the metal gate. I'll give the signal when I'm successful."

I didn't want everyone hanging out so close while I tried to get in. We'd just make a bigger, easier target.

Roarke accompanied me to the grate, but there was nothing I could do about that. No chance he'd leave my side.

We hurried to the edge of the wall and pressed our bodies against it. Fortunately, at the back of the castle, there weren't any sentries. I crept along the stone till I reached the river, then leaned over and pressed my hand to the metal grate.

I called on my new power over metal, envisioning melting the iron. It flamed red in my mind, but nothing happened with the actual grate. I tried harder, forcing my magic toward it. Sweat broke out on my brow.

"Not working," I whispered.

"Protective spell," Roarke said.

I sighed and pulled back. We'd been afraid of this. It'd been easy to escape because there weren't any protective charms preventing that. The inhabitants would need the option to escape if there was a siege. But getting in? That was a lot harder.

We'd decided that Roarke wouldn't try to break the charm because if he punched the iron grate, it'd be loud enough to alert the guards.

I pressed my fingertips to the charm at my neck. "Cass? Send Aidan."

"On it." Her voice echoed quietly.

A few minutes later, a small bird flew up and landed on the ground next to us. A sparrow. Golden light glowed from the bird and it transformed, taking the shape of a man. A moment later, Aidan stood in front of us.

"Protective charm?" he asked.

"Yep."

He dug into his pocket and pulled out a small silver charm. A spell stripper. I'd seen him use it before. It was a nifty—and rare—piece of magic that could remove protective enchantments. It was damned hard to get your hands on one, but Aidan owned a security company so it was sort of in his line of work.

Aidan leaned over the river and ran the spell stripper around the edges of the grate.

I waited, breath held.

He leaned back and looked at me, brows drawn. "No good. The charm is too strong. Unlike anything I've ever seen."

Though disappointed, I wasn't surprised. This couldn't be that easy.

"Plan C," I said.

He nodded and shifted, transforming back into a sparrow and flying across the forest to our friends.

Nerves raced across my skin as I looked at Roarke. "Ready for this?"

He reached out and pulled me close, pressing a hard kiss to my lips.

I savored the contact, gripping him hard. Being close to him made this whole thing seem easier. More possible. The evil of the forest couldn't break the little bubble of safety that formed when I was with him. Together, we could take on anything.

With my *deirfiúr* at our backs?

We were invincible.

I pulled away from Roarke, then looked at my watch. "Two minutes," I said.

He nodded.

I dug into my pocket and pulled out two small blue vials. I passed one to Roarke and we drank. It was sweet—far tastier than the invisibility potion—and a warm rush flowed through my muscles. The potion was a clever addition from Connor, who'd given a couple to Cass. Something new he'd been working on that was meant to strengthen the drinker's system so that it could withstand injury and potions.

I sure hoped it worked.

We stood in silence as the concoction coursed through our bodies. My chest vibrated with tension as I waited, my gaze following the undulating flow of the dark mist that covered the ground. Any time a particularly thick patch brushed against my ankles, I shivered.

Finally, it was time.

I called upon my Ubilaz demon power, letting it flow free for the first time since I'd learned to control it.

Since we couldn't break in, we were going to have to be taken in.

We were bait.

And the best bait was very attractive. Fortunately, my most despised power was now becoming useful.

As I let the Ubilaz demon power fly free, attracting whatever demons were nearby, I knelt by the river and pretended to fiddle with the grate.

A few moments later, a shout sounded from above. Demons dropped down from the wall all around us. Five, all different species. But every one was big and had magic that smelled awful. Rotten eggs, mold, garbage, and vomit.

What a lovely bunch. Like a bouquet of roses for the devil.

I turned off my Ubilaz demon power and jumped to my feet, slowly drawing my sword from the ether. Roarke threw a punch at the nearest demon. It landed, knocking the beast to its back. His next strike was slower, intentionally so.

A demon jumped him, tackling him about the waist.

Roarke went down easy.

I swiped my blade at the demon nearest me, but he dodged and lunged for me, slapping a damp rag over my face. As expected, the familiar smell of the sedative hit me. But it didn't have any effect.

Thank you, Connor.

I sagged against the demon, pretending to be knocked out. I dropped my sword, then sent it back into the ether, hoping the demons didn't notice. Through barely-open eyes, I watched another demon jump on Roarke and pull the same trick. Roarke struggled, but feebly.

Dumb demon wasn't even smart enough to realize who he was up against.

After a last halfhearted twitch—which I felt was a bit overkill—Roarke sagged against his captor.

The one holding me slung me over his shoulder. The air whooshed out of me as my stomach collided with his sharp bones. Pain radiated through my midsection, but I choked back a groan.

Once again, three demons had to carry Roarke. We made our way slowly around the castle wall. Carefully, I called upon my power over ice. The air was chilly, so a little snow wouldn't be too amiss. At least the sky was kinda cloudy. Hopefully, it would better hide my friends. They might be invisible, but they still made footprints.

I called down the snow, and snowflakes began to fall all around us, softly at first, then more and more until we were in a veritable blizzard.

"Buzzard's balls, I thought we had another day before snow," muttered the demon who carried me.

Little do you know, buzzard balls.

They tromped up to the main gate, their footfalls heavy on the wooden bridge that traversed a gap in the stone.

"Open up! We've retrieved the Demise!"

I stiffened, then caught myself, trying to relax slowly so he wouldn't notice me. But my heart raced.

Even this lackey called me the Demise?

This was bad business.

Slowly, the iron gate crept upward, creaking with every inch. As the demons stomped inside, I prayed to fate that this plan would work. Because suddenly, it felt *really* risky.

I hadn't seen this part of the fortress before. Through slitted eyes, I saw that the main courtyard was large and barren. Above, demons whispered. Were they on the ramparts, controlling the gate? I couldn't see without blowing my cover, so I bounced along on the back of the demon who carried me, biding my time and praying this wasn't a dumb idea.

Soon, they hauled us through the door of what I assumed was the main building. The light was dim and the large foyer empty. The door swung shut behind us.

The demon who held me jerked and grunted, as if he'd been punched in the stomach.

Go time!

I thrashed, managing to fall off the demon's shoulder as someone hit him. I crashed to the ground, unable to see my friends but able to see the havoc they wreaked on the five demons who had carried us. It was like a strange action sequence, watching them get beaten up by invisible people. Hopefully the demons on the ramparts wouldn't hear the fight.

Roarke had gotten free of his captors and broken the neck of one. He tossed the body aside and looked for another, but my friends had taken care of the rest.

I dug into my pocket and pulled out my vial of invisibility potion, then choked it down.

Tasted just as gross this time as the last. I grimaced and changed my original flavor assessment from mud to monkey butt. I'd never licked a monkey's butt and didn't intend to, but I'd bet my books on it tasting just like this.

As the shivery sensation ran through my limbs, my friends became visible, courtesy of the potion that allowed me to see the others who had taken the same elixir. All the demons lay on the ground, dead and quickly disappearing.

Cass was retrieving one of her handy daggers from the chest of a fallen demon, while Nix dusted her hands and grinned at me.

"Not bad, eh?" she asked.

"Went off without a hitch." I turned to examine the room. It was empty, but it wouldn't stay that way. "We'd better get a move on."

"Yes," Roarke said.

I called on my dragon sense, feeding it my desire to find Draka's source egg. It tugged weakly, toward the back exit. But it felt...weird. Here, but not.

That couldn't be good.

I pointed toward the exterior exit. "That way."

We hurried toward the door. I pushed it open slowly and peered outside. No one.

Just an empty courtyard with a ramshackle garden.

"Weird for a fortress," Cass said.

"Don't like it," I muttered.

"My dragon sense pulls that way, too," Nix said. "But it's weak."

"Same," I said. "Let's try."

We hurried out into the garden, which was full of overgrown plants of all varieties. Most were dingy green or almost dead, lending the place a creepy air. The same black mist that had been in the forest hovered over the ground here, doing the plants no favors. The back wall of the garden was made entirely of thick brown thorns. My dragon sense tugged toward it.

Of course it did. Looked like something straight out of the dark part of a fairy tale, so of course we were headed in that direction.

There was a small gap in the thorns, right in the middle.

"We have to enter," I said.

"Perfect," Cass muttered. "Always with the creepy shit."

We neared the wall of thorns. Each pointy bit was at least six inches long. More like a wall of little daggers than thorny vines. I reached out to touch one, but Roarke grabbed my hand.

"Don't. They could be poisonous," he said.

"Good point." I withdrew my hand, then slipped into the gap in the wall.

It expanded out to form a wide corridor. The walls and ceiling were all made of the thick, dead thorny vines. Roarke followed me in, then Cass, Nix, and Aidan.

"Bad news bears, this," Cass murmured.

"No kidding." We started down the corridor, moving quickly in case the demons followed. They would, eventually.

Soon we hit a split in the path. We were given three choices.

I gasped. "It's a labyrinth."

"Of course," Nix said. "That's why our dragon sense is so weird and weak. The egg is so well protected. Almost hidden."

"My dragon sense tugs left," I said.

"Mine too," Nix and Cass said in unison.

"Left it is," Aidan said.

We set off down the pathway, jogging to keep ahead of any demons who might be in pursuit. A thorny branch snapped off the wall and nearly hit me in the face. I barely managed to dodge, ducking low and letting the thing whip over my head.

Another came from the left, nicking me in the side.

Acid pain bloomed, making me gasp.

Through the pain, I felt Nix's magic swell on the air, carrying the scent of flowers that was so out of place in this hell hole.

"Del! Catch!" Nix's voice.

I turned, catching the long, thin metal shield that Nix shoved at me. The weight dragged my arm down, but I stiffened it and shielded myself. She conjured more as the vines began to whip out at us.

I turned and ran, letting the shield take the brunt of the blows. The vines slammed into the shield, some of the thorns breaking off in the metal and poking through. We sprinted for ages until my side pinched, and I was weak from the pain of the first vine blow.

By the time the attacks ceased, I was panting and sweating. We stumbled to a halt, gasping.

"Quick thinking, Nix," Cass said.

"Thank you," Roarke said.

"You're the—" I bent over as the pain in my side sliced through me.

"You were hit." Worry was thick in Roarke's voice.

I pressed a hand to my side and winced. "Not bad, just one thorn."

"They were big thorns." Aidan approached my side. "Let me see."

I raised my shirt, then gasped at the sight. Blood poured from a puncture wound in my side as if I'd been stabbed with a dagger. Sure felt like it.

"That's deep." Aidan knelt and held a hand up by my wound. "Mind?"

"Not at all." I chuckled, then winced.

He hovered his hand over the wound, and warmth flowed from his palm. Slowly, I relaxed, the pain leaching from me as the wound closed.

I felt almost entirely better by the time he stood and said, "That's the best I can do. I think there was probably poison in it, but the potion you took earlier helped fight it."

Thank you, Connor. "Thanks, Aidan." The wound was now just a red mark with a little slice through it. But the worst was gone. "Let's head on."

We picked up our jog again, with Roarke next to me and my three friends slightly behind. The air in the labyrinth smelled rotten, forcing me to breathe shallowly. I'd never been claustrophobic before, but the ceiling of thorns over my head was giving me the willies.

A buzzing started, but I thought it was my imagination. Then a wasp came, flying straight at me. My eyes focused on it when it was only a few feet away. I dodged, but it became stuck in a flying wisp of my hair.

I shook my head to free it. It escaped, and I immediately forgot about the little jerk when I caught sight of the massive horde of wasps coming straight at us. Each one was the size of a hamster. The little guy who'd been stuck in my hair was just an emissary.

"Poisonous mega-wasps," Roarke said. "Underworld species."

"Shit!" I'd only heard of them as a nightmare specie, whose venom immobilized you while they devoured you alive.

"Duck!" Cass yelled.

I crouched low, Roarke copying me. Above our heads, massive flames roared through the air. I glanced up, my face warmed by the blaze. Cass and Aidan were shooting fire from their palms, obliterating the wasps as they neared.

I was damned glad to have them on our side.

A few moments later, the fire extinguished, and they lowered their hands. A fine gray dust littered the path in front of us.

I sagged, panting. "Good job, guys."

"Yeah." Nix wiped sweat from her brow. "I really thought we were—"

Pounding footsteps sounded from behind us, and Nix snapped her mouth shut.

Roarke and I leapt to our feet and turned. Braced, we waited. My heart thundered, pounding in my ears like the beat of a thousand drummers. A moment later, a group of a dozen demons appeared about thirty yards away, racing toward us. I called on my magic, ready to hurl an icicle at the oncoming monsters.

Then logic stole in.

The corridor was wide. The demons were going single file, as if they'd been trained to do so in some deadly demon circus.

I caught my friends' gazes and gestured to the sides of the corridor. We pressed ourselves against it, close enough that I could feel the barest prickle of thorns poking my jacket. I held my breath as the demons ran past, praying they'd be able to report back to their master that the labyrinth was clear. That should buy us some time.

As the last one passed, that same little wasp appeared, flying straight past my eyes, so fast I could feel the brush of wings. I flinched, the finest squeak escaping my lips.

The last demon turned, suspicion on his ugly gray face. He had massive horns and a nose similar to a pig's—which was an insult to pigs.

His comrades kept running, but he stood still, staring at us—unable to see through our invisibility potions, but clearly knowing something was up. He opened his mouth as if to call for the other demons. I fired up an icicle and hurled it at his face before he got a sound out.

It pierced him straight through the mouth, gruesome enough that my stomach turned. As his knees collapsed out from under him, Roarke raced forward and caught him, silencing his fall.

My heart was lodged in my throat as the other demons turned a corner up ahead, not realizing the silent drama that had gone on behind them.

"Quick thinking," Cass whispered.

"Thanks."

Roarke lowered the body to the ground, then stood. We waited a moment to give the other demons time to get far ahead of us, standing in silence while watching the demon's body to see how long it would take to disappear back to the Underworld.

Finally, the body began to fade out.

"Let's go," I said.

We set off running, keeping our footfalls silent on the dirt beneath us. We came to the path that the demons had followed, but my dragon sense pulled me straight ahead. That way was definitely darker, as if the thorny branches were thicker and wouldn't allow sunlight in.

"Don't love the look of that direction," Cass said.

"Means it's the right one," Nix said. "It always seems to be the scary shit."

We hurried down the path, which was narrower than the one we'd left but still at least six feet wide. Shadows grew in front of us, along with a fresh smell. Like a lake. It was so out of place that my stride faltered.

The shadows coalesced to form a glittering blue wave. It filled the corridor, roaring toward us.

My skin chilled as my mind blanked. Then an idea roared to the surface.

I called upon my power over ice and flung my hands out, forcing the magic toward the oncoming wave. At first, nothing happened. I gave it more, sweat breaking out on my brow.

The wave slowed, turning to slush. I fed it more power, imagining it freezing solid. My muscles shook with the strain. A moment later, it froze, an ice sculpture of oncoming doom.

"Niiiiice," Cass murmured.

"Saved our bacon," Aidan said.

I swallowed hard, inspecting the icy wave. It formed a thick wall over the entire passageway. "Now we just need to get through it."

"I'll give it a go." Roarke stepped forward, and the gray tornado of his magic formed around him. It obscured him briefly before he appeared again, shifted into his demon form. He was careful to keep his wings tucked in close as he approached the frozen wave.

He pulled his fist back and slammed it forward, using his massive magical strength to put several large cracks in the ice. The blow should have broken his knuckles, but his gift prevented it. He plowed his fist forward again, deepening the cracks. It took several blows, but eventually, the wave crumbled in a pile of icy shards and boulders.

"Nicely done." I grinned at him, then climbed over the shards of ice.

It went on for ages, slippery piles that we scrambled over. It would have been enough water to drown us.

By the time we were on the other side, my hands were frozen.

"Pretty solid labyrinth, eh?" Nix said.

"Not bad." An understatement.

I started jogging again, ready to get the hell out of here. We'd handled it pretty well so far, but the stress of what might come next was starting to wear on me. Not to mention, good luck streaks could only last so long.

We ran for at least ten minutes, following my dragon sense down twists and turns and outshoots. When the dark shadow prowled out from another corridor, I was actually beginning to think we might be near the end.

How freaking wrong.

I slowed, taking in the massive shape in front of me. It was like a dog, but lumpy and strange, with stunted wings on its back. It prowled closer, the shadows receding from its form.

I swallowed hard, my skin chilled. Scaly grey skin covered a monstrous beast on four legs. It was like something from my worst nightmares. Massive fangs protruded from its mouth, dripping what I assumed was poison, and its claws were at least eight inches long and tipped with an oily black substance.

"Underworld beast." Roarke's voice was gravelly in his demon form. "A Chironera."

The beast growled, dipping low on its front legs as if ready to pounce. Roarke stepped in front of us and flared his wings. His magic surged, nearly bringing me to my knees. I hadn't felt it this strong since I'd met him. The scent of sandalwood drove out the rotten smell in the air while the taste of wine exploded on my tongue. His form glowed blue with his aura.

I couldn't see the beast, but its growling stopped.

I peeked around Roarke's hip in the gap created by his wing. The beast was doing some sort of weird bow, its head bent.

The demons hadn't recognized Roarke in his human form, but this beast recognized the Warden of the Underworld right now. Hard to miss him, with all that power rolling out. Thank fates.

"Step aside." Roarke's voice rumbled with power.

The beast stepped aside. Roarke went to stand in front of it as we passed single file. The scent of rotten meat spilled from the monster's mouth as I walked by, but the floral aroma of Nix's magic surged. I glanced behind to see her conjure a big steak and lay it at the beast's feet.

I grinned, loving my *deirfiúr* more in that moment than I almost ever had.

The beast blinked at Nix, then chomped on the steak. We continued on, Roarke picking up the back and leaving the monster to enjoy its dinner.

The shadows in the passage grew darker as we ran. At first, I thought it was just the lack of light, but then I realized it was a strange black mist. Like the fog out in the woods. When we came to a crossroads, I grew woozy.

It was the mist. It had to be. I turned to my friends, wanting to take hands in case we lost one another.

But they were nowhere. "Guys?"

Silence. Just more black mist, slowly obscuring the thorny walls around me.

"Roarke? Cass? Nix? Aidan?"

Nothing.

Just like back in Wales, when the white mist had swallowed everyone.

For fate's sake, I couldn't get a break.

CHAPTER THIRTEEN

My heartbeat thudded in my ears. This was the second time I'd lost my friends, but I had a feeling it wouldn't be as easy to find them this go-round.

I drew my sword from the ether, not because I heard someone coming, but because it was like my sharp, pointy security blanket. I wasn't quite as alone in the mist if I had it in my hand. For good measure, I called upon my Phantom power, letting the cold magic flow through me and turn me blue and transparent and hoping it would attract my friends to me like before.

I wouldn't put any money on this trick working in the thick black mist that surrounded me, but I had to try.

I gave it a moment, then called on my dragon sense, asking it to take me to Draka's egg and praying everyone else could find it, too. It was a good plan; otherwise, I could be searching for Nix while she went away from me, searching for Cass.

The magic tugged around my waist and I followed, keeping my sword held at an angle in front of me so that it would bump into the thorns before I did.

I turned left, then right, weaving through the labyrinth and praying my dragon sense led me true. By the time the mist cleared, worry for my friends had formed a balloon inside my chest. It nearly suffocated me.

I stepped into a small clearing where the thorny walls had expanded outward. A heavy stone door was in front of me, but none of my friends. I crept forward, pressing my hand to the door and trying to feel if there were any magical signatures that would indicate enemies inside.

I felt nothing but the pull of Draka's source egg.

Slowly, I pushed open the heavy door. The air inside was cool and dim. Silent.

I slipped in, my gaze widening. I was in a massive domed room. A pool of white light filled the center, shining down from a crystal at the top of the dome. A little window allowed sunlight to flow in, hit the crystal, and then spread out. The rest of the room was dim.

But what caught my eye was the pedestal with Draka's blue source egg sitting atop it. My fingertips itched to race forward and grab it, but the glowing white light made goosebumps stand up on my skin.

I approached it slowly, keeping all my senses alert for the magical signature of the light. Draka had said her egg was held captive in a trap. Was this the trap?

I'd bet all the books in my trove that it was.

When I neared the light, I knocked on my head, then reached out a single finger to poke the light. Just as I was about to touch it, the door behind me creaked open.

Praying for my friends but expecting the worst, I turned, my breath held.

In the doorway stood a Shadow. The figure was shaped roughly like a man in a cloak—the Grim Reaper, to be honest—but the cloak was semi-transparent and flowed like mist around his ankles.

Instinctively, I threw an icicle at him. It hadn't worked a week ago, when I'd walked through the portal into the tower from my childhood, but I had to try. Again, it sailed straight through him.

Damn it.

"Is that the best you can do?" The Shadow's voice was as sibilant as a snake's hiss.

I raised my sword, remembering how it had wounded him a week ago.

"Who are you?" I demanded. "What do you want with me?"

"Everything." The Shadow whipped out a hand, and a long snake-shaped wisp of fog snapped toward me. It wrapped around my ankle, yanking me off my feet.

I slammed into the ground, barely keeping my grip on my sword. He shouldn't have been able to grasp me in my Phantom form. But then, my Phantom sword shouldn't affect him, and it had.

We could hurt each other in our weird ethereal bodies.

I did a sit-up and sliced at the wisp of fog, cleaving it in two with my blade. I scrambled up as he whipped out another coil. I lunged, dodging it by a millimeter, and called upon my ice power.

I pressed my palm to the ground and forced my magic into the stone, envisioning a great wall of ice between me and the Shadow. It grew quickly, glimmering and blue, to about ten feet overhead and ten feet wide.

It wouldn't do much, other than give me time to plan, and I prayed that was enough. My mind raced. I could try to get Draka's egg, but that white light would probably trap me if it had trapped her Phantom dragon egg.

The Shadow shot another wisp of fog at me. It struck the ice, bouncing back. But his next shot whipped around the side of the ice wall. I dodged, but was too slow. It curled around my waist, pulling me to the side.

I sliced it off with my sword, but another whip followed it, winding around my thigh. Then another on my arm.

I cut them off, but another flew at me, enveloping my ankle.

Shit! He was too fast. And I was trapped.

He stood in front of the only exit, his black cloak whipping in a nonexistent wind, tendrils of smoke lashing out toward me.

I glanced behind me at Draka's egg.

There was only one thing left to do…

Save her.

I was caught, but she didn't have to be. Who knew if my plan would work, but I had to try. And maybe my friends would find me in time to save me.

I sliced off the tendril of shadow that tugged at my ankle, then raced for the pedestal holding Draka's egg. As soon as I entered the white light, my limbs grew sluggish. It was like running through water, as if the light were holding me captive.

The only benefit was that the Shadow's wispy tendrils couldn't reach me in the light. They snapped against it, reflected. I was sweating by the time I reached Draka's egg and grabbed it off the pedestal.

The Shadow yelled, but I ignored it. Focus was the only thing keeping me going as my limbs became heavier and heavier, affected by the crystal hanging high above. I was moving pretty fast, but it took everything in me.

Her magic swelled against my hand. I could almost feel something beating inside the egg. Like dragon wings. It gave me a boost of strength, and I surged toward the edge of the light. By the time I made it, I was on my knees. I toppled over and shoved the egg out of the light.

It rolled on the stone floor and glowed brilliant blue, bursting with light. The glow slammed out into the room, then disappeared.

I tried to drag myself across the stone to escape the light trap, but I was stuck—as if someone had superglued my belly to the floor.

Now *this* was the dignified end I'd always hoped for.

Slowly, I managed to turn my head. The Shadow approached, skirting the edge of the light, careful not to touch it. When he finally stood over me, I could only catch a glimpse of him out of the corner of my eye, looming over me. The Grim Reaper come to deliver the death blow.

"The time has come," the Shadow intoned.

"Asshole. Is that the best you've got? Some vague, ominous bullshit?" The words came out slurred and slow, a product of the magic that trapped me. It weakened even my jaw muscles.

"You should be grateful. You will take your place among us as queen."

I sputtered a laugh. "Sure, queen of what?"

"The world, once we are free."

Now I really started laughing, though it sounded like some weird record played too slow. And I didn't know why I was laughing, because it certainly wasn't funny. But it was ridiculous. I was trapped here, glued to the floor like a piece of dropped baloney, listening to this creeper spell out some horrible future in which I was *queen*.

But the worst part was, part of me *liked* the idea of being queen. It made me vaguely queasy, but that part was there.

"Go to hell," I muttered.

"Not a problem. We'll go soon enough. Once we're—"

The door creaked open. I could just barely see out of the corner of my eye.

My heart dropped. A man carried in a struggling woman. For a moment, I thought it was Roarke carrying Cass. But he looked different. Shorter. Paler.

Holy fates, was that his brother?

Other figures came through the door, distracting me. Demons carrying Nix, Aidan, and finally Roarke. It took several demons to contain Roarke and Aidan. Roarke was beaten to hell, his form limp with one wing broken and cuts pouring blood. Like he'd put up a fight and the demons hadn't liked it. The others didn't look great either. More demons crowded in behind, which wasn't surprising. It would have taken a lot to bring my friends down.

Hope disappeared.

All captured. Too many enemies. And this damned light that had me pinned like a bug.

Roarke twitched, regaining consciousness and lifting his head. His gaze darted around the room, falling on the man who looked like him.

From all the way across the room, I could see his eyes widen. Shock, joy, then despair.

It *was* his brother. *Oh, shit.*

And he was on the side of the Shadows, the mysterious enemy from my past who had placed the curse on my mind. What did they want with me? And why was he on their side?

"It seems we're all together now." The Shadow's voice hissed. "But I won't be needing your companions."

"So let them go," I said.

He laughed. "Hardly. Kill them!"

"No!" I thrashed. Or tried to. I was stuck solid, unable to escape.

Roarke's brother dropped Cass to the ground and reached for his sword. As he was reaching, she scrambled up and darted away. Hope flared in my chest until a demon jumped her and took her to the ground.

A blue light surged through the door, massive and so bright it nearly drowned out the white light that trapped me. It coalesced to form the shape of a dragon that hurtled for the ceiling.

Draka!

She'd escaped!

She flew for the ceiling, avoiding the white light that trapped me, and whacked her tail at the crystal charm that was creating the bewitched light. It sailed through the air and crashed against the stone wall, shattering.

Immediately, the light that trapped me faded. Strength returned to my limbs. The superglue disappeared. I leapt up, sword gripped in my hand.

Draka swooped toward the guards holding my friends, knocking them over. Bodies tumbled and my friends scrambled free, lighting up the room with their magic. Cass hurled fire while Nix threw arrows. Aidan shifted and Roarke raced for his brother, running because his damaged wing would not fly.

I left them to it, lunging for the Shadow. I collided with him, taking him down.

Just touching his ethereal form made me shudder—probably how folks felt when they touched me. He had no face, just more shadow in the vague shape of a cloaked head.

He grasped my shoulder, but I swung my sword, severing his arm.

He hissed as smoke rose from the wound. I stabbed him through the shoulder, pinning him.

"Tell me what your plan is!" I demanded.

"Never!" There was such vehemence in his voice that I believed him.

"Then I have no use for you." I withdrew the sword and stabbed it through his neck.

He hissed louder; more smoke billowed up. As he faded, he hissed, "We are legion, we are more."

The words disappeared on the air, along with his body.

Had I killed him? I thought so, but I didn't have time to worry about it. I hopped up, taking in the scene around me.

My friends fought demons—over forty of them. Nix had conjured a sandbag barricade. From behind it, she and Cass fired arrows and flames. Aidan had shifted into a griffin and was flying through the air alongside Draka, decapitating demons with his beak. Blood sprayed with every chomp.

Roarke was stuck on the ground with his broken wing, but he was in the middle of the melee, tearing off demon heads left and right. He moved so fast I almost couldn't see him.

But his brother was gone.

Ran off like a coward.

I raced toward Cass and Nix, stowing my sword in the ether and calling upon my ice magic. Side by side, we hurled our weapons, killing demon after demon. With Draka's help, we had a chance.

Soon, the demons overran our barricade. They surged between us, separating us. I drew my sword from the ether, going corporeal so it would strike. I lunged for the demon nearest me, sinking my blade into his stomach. I pulled it free and swiped out at the demon next to him, removing his head.

Pain sliced through my shoulder and I turned, gagging at the tearing feeling of a blade pulling free. A spindly gray demon stood behind me, a wicked looking sword in his hand. It dripped my blood.

Oh, for fate's sake, this being human thing sucked. I called upon my Phantom power, letting the cool magic wash through me. It was time to practice some close-range icicle warfare, because I wasn't keen on getting stabbed again.

As blood poured down my back, I didn't think I had too many stabbings left in me today.

The spindly demon swung his blade at me, but it sailed right through my ethereal form. I charged up a tiny icicle, no more than twelve inches long, and sent it right into his chest. His milky eyes widened, and he tumbled back. I whirled, searching for another demon.

There was one coming up behind me, a massive demon with muscles on top of muscles. His serrated sword was raised to cleave my head in two.

No, thanks.

I hit him with another icicle, but it bounced off. Too small to pierce his thick chest, unlike my success with the skinny demon. This was the downside to the close-range icicle warfare. I called upon a bigger icicle, and this one plunged halfway into his chest.

He stopped, teetering on thick legs, and I kicked him over. At my side, Cass had lit up half a dozen demons, and Nix had fired arrows into the eyes of four more. Aidan's discarded demon heads littered the ground, while Roarke's broken bodies were piled up against the wall.

Draka picked up the last demon and chucked him into the wall.

The room fell silent, the only sound our panting breaths.

"Well, that was something," Nix said.

"Yeah." I sought out Roarke, who looked slightly shell-shocked. His wing looked better, as if it'd just been pulled out of joint before and had now been shoved back in, but his expression was still blown apart. "We need to get out of here."

"Yeah." Cass limped over. "There've gotta be more demons in this place, and I'm in no shape to get into it with them right now."

Neither was I. In fact, I was about to be puddle-shaped, because blood loss from the wound in my shoulder was starting to make me woozy.

CHAPTER FOURTEEN

It was, by far, the weirdest family dinner I'd ever attended. In fairness, I'd never been to a family dinner unless you could count pizza with Del and Nix, but I'd seen them on TV and they did not look like this.

We were all scattered around Roarke's kitchen, drinking wine and chatting. It'd been a full day since the battle at the fortress in Germany. I'd needed the time to recover from my wounds, and so had my friends. There'd been everything from burns and cuts to broken bones.

But we were healed now, mostly, and Roarke was making us dinner while the Allman brothers played on the stereo. Badass Warden of the Underworld was pulling lasagna out of the oven while Connor worked on a pastry on the other side of the counter. Emile and Roarke stood, discussing something intently while the two little rats, Ralph and Rufus, slept on Emile's shoulders. Claire, Cass, and Nix played some kind of drinking game called Sink the Bismarck.

"You've created a lovely life for yourself," Draka said from beside me.

I glanced at her and couldn't help but feel my chest warm at her words. She was the closest thing I had to a mother who cared about me. Right now, she was in her *human* form, though she still looked like a Phantom with that strange, ageless quality only she possessed.

"They're great, aren't they?" I said. "But couldn't you hang around now that you're free?"

She shook her head. "I cannot. With our dwindling numbers, Phantom dragons are weaker. It's how the Shadows managed to catch me in the first place. Sometimes my power falters. I must return to our cave to regenerate my strength."

"Of course."

"But I'll be there for you if you need me."

"I know." I frowned into my mug of red wine. "And I'm going to need you, aren't I? Whatever is coming is bad."

"I think you have an idea."

Yeah. Me, queen of some demons destroying Earth. *Super great.*

"Why did the Shadows place the curse on my mind that made it hard for me to control my power?" I asked. "Wouldn't they want me to use my power to help them?"

"I think they doubt you. They didn't want you to use your power against them, so they tried to block that."

"They just want to catch me and use me. Or, some mysterious power that I have."

"Yes."

"What monsters. Why did my family align with them? Why did they want me to play this role?"

"You're the only one who could. And they aligned with the demons for the same reason most people do anything. They wanted power. If the demons succeeded, they stood to play an important role in the new world order."

"But they didn't get it. They're dead." The memory of the abandoned castles in Wales sank my heart. "How?"

"They were playing a game they weren't equipped for. After they gave you to the man you call the Monster, the Shadows and their demon minions were enraged. They thought your parents were trying to hide you from them."

My heart leapt. "Were they?"

Draka's face turned sad. "No. I'm sorry. Your parents gave you to the Monster because they truly thought he could help you fulfill your part in the Shadow's plans. But the Shadows didn't believe them."

"So they killed them."

"There is no happy ending to the story of your parents. They were cold, hard people. They died the way they deserved to." The hardness in her voice made me blink back tears. She was able to be collected about it. I wasn't. They were still my family, and I'd long harbored fantasies of them being alive and wonderful.

Draka's hand touched my shoulder, warming my skin. I could feel her love through her touch. A smile tugged at my lips. I did have her though.

"Why are you my guardian?" I asked.

"Because I wanted to be. My kind has lived on your family's ancestral land for millennia. For a long time, we didn't like your family much."

"Considering my parents, it's hard not to see why."

She smiled. "But I saw you in your tower one day while I was flying. I saw how hard you tried and how sad you were. Our numbers were dwindling at that time. We were down to four Phantom dragons, myself included, so I understood your struggle. I connected with you. Very rarely, a Phantom dragon bonds with a Phantom."

"And we bonded? Is that why you were able to send me a message with the blue light?"

"Yes. It is not easy, but with someone I truly care about, I can manage it. And thank you for saving me, though you did not follow my directions." She smiled.

"Of course. I'm glad I found you."

"Me, too." She squeezed my shoulder. "You have the strength for what is coming. You know that, don't you?"

"I hope you're right."

"But you're going to need more power."

"I know. I don't have the power my parents hoped I would, do I?" My magic was being revealed talent by talent, but there was that last big question.

She shook her head. "Not yet. You are strong and rare, but there is more for you still. Both the power you will take and the power that will grow."

Taking must mean stealing it from demons. As for the power that would grow... "Do you know what it is?"

"I do not. But it is dangerous, I am sure of that. Or so many demons wouldn't want you."

"Yeah, I figured." My grip tightened on my cup. "What about my home? I don't think of it as mine, not really, but I want those damned demons out of there."

"You can reclaim it. But you'll have to seal off the portal to the Underworld if you want to keep the demons out. It's been like that for centuries, ever since your line made a pact with the Underworld."

"So it's more than just dusting and fixing the windows, huh?" I laughed. "I was hoping to sell it as a ski resort."

Draka smiled. "I am not very good with humor, but I doubt that."

"Yeah, I don't know what I would do with it. But I don't want the damned demons to have it."

"Then you must fight them, or they will overrun the earth."

"Do you mean they are trying to escape the Underworld?"

She shrugged. "It's my current theory, but I have no proof."

Damn. That was bad.

"Dinner's up!" Roarke called.

Draka turned to me and smiled. "That is my signal to leave."

"You won't stay for dinner?"

"No. I do not eat your type of food. I only wanted an opportunity to say goodbye to you. Hopefully, I will see you again."

"You'd better count on it."

She smiled and we embraced. I watched her walk out onto the patio and transform into a dragon, and then take off. When I turned back to the table, my friends were waiting.

I joined Nix and Cass, taking the seat between them. They each reached for one of my hands and squeezed. I smiled at them both, grateful to fate that they were at my side.

Later that night, after everyone had left, Roarke and I sat in front of the fire drinking mugs of red wine. I played with the lucky talismans around my neck as the fire crackled, sending a welcoming glow over the rug and onto the gleaming wooden table.

"Draka said I have a lovely life." I looked up at him and took his hand. "I think she was right."

"She *was* right." His gaze met mine, and he squeezed my hand. "You make my life better."

"We've only known each other a few weeks."

"Best few weeks of my life."

I grinned, then leaned up and kissed him.

When I pulled away, he said, "I knew you were special, Del. You're just proving how special."

"I hope I can keep proving it. Because there's a lot at stake." My mind flashed back to the moment in the fortress when I'd seen Roarke's brother. Between recovering and sleeping, we hadn't had a chance to talk about it. "Do you think that really was your brother?"

Roarke's gaze turned weary. Hope and despair flickered on his face. "It was. He disappeared before I could get to him. I don't know how he escaped the Order. They were supposed to be able to contain him."

"And now he's teamed up with the Shadows. Who want me for some kind of terrible plot."

"Yes. But I'm going to find him. I have to."

I nodded, staring into the flames. "Of course."

"And whatever they have planned, we'll stop it." Roarke tugged me closer to his side, and I snuggled against him. "Don't worry."

"Hard not to." I sucked in a deep breath. "But you're right. We've got this. I'm prepared to do what it takes. Whatever it takes."

"You're talking about your powers, aren't you?"

"Yeah. If I have to steal demon powers to have what I need to fight this, I'll do it." I'd been scared before, and hell, I was still scared, but I was willing to face what was coming. To stand up and fight.

And whatever my *other* power was that hadn't come into fruition yet? Well, I'd deal with it when it came.

"You can do it, Del. I believe in you." He leaned down and pressed a kiss to my head.

I wrapped my arms around his waist and squeezed, enjoying every second of being with him. Of being with my friends tonight, all around a dinner table like the family we were. My parents might have turned out to be monsters, and there was no going back. But I didn't want to go back to an imaginary past. I wanted to go forward, into the life I'd created.

And I believed him—I could do this. I had to do this.

Because I sure as hell didn't want to find out what would happen if I failed.

THANK YOU FOR READING!

I hope you enjoyed reading this book as much as I enjoyed writing it. Reviews are so helpful to authors. I really appreciate all reviews, both positive and negative. If you want to leave one, you can do so at Amazon or GoodReads.

AUTHOR'S NOTE

Hi! *Magic Revealed* was so much fun to write. I hope you enjoyed it. If you've read any of my author's notes before, you'll know I'm an archaeologist as well as a writer. This influences my books enormously and is why so many of them have scenes set at historic sites. This particular book doesn't have as many historical or mythological elements because it was so focused on discovering Del's past, but there was one little thing I included.

The ghostly white wolves who help Del when she is near her home in the Welsh mountains are based on the Cŵn Annwn, the ghostly hounds of the Welsh underworld, Annwn. There are many aspects to their mythology. They're associated with the Wild Hunt, which is featured in many European mythologies. The Wild Hunt is said to be a group of supernatural hunters passing in the night, and if you see them, it can foretell catastrophe. Also, the bark or growl of the Cŵn Annwn can indicate that death is coming, and in some stories, they accompany the dead to the underworld.

That's it for the historical influences in *Magic Revealed*. However, one of the most important things about this book is how Del and her *deirfiúr* treat artifacts and their business, Ancient Magic. If you've read my author's notes before, you've read the next part. But it's important to me, so I'm including this for anyone who hasn't had a chance to read it.

As I'm sure you know, archaeology isn't quite like Indiana Jones (for which I'm both grateful and bitterly disappointed). Sure, it's exciting and full of travel. However, booby-traps are not as common as I expected. Total number of booby-traps I have encountered in my career: zero. Still hoping, though.

When I chose to write a series about archaeology and treasure hunting, I knew I had a careful line to tread. There is a big difference between these two activities. As much as I value artifacts, they are not treasure. Not even the gold artifacts. They are pieces of our history that contain valuable information, and as such, they belong to all of us. Every artifact that is excavated should be properly conserved and stored in a museum so that everyone can have access to our history. No one single person can own history, and I believe very strongly that individuals should not own artifacts. Treasure hunting is the pursuit of artifacts for personal gain.

So why did I make Del and her *deirfiúr* treasure hunters? I'd have loved to call them archaeologists, but nothing about Cass's work is like archaeology. Archaeology is a very laborious, painstaking process—

and it certainly doesn't involve selling artifacts. That wouldn't work for the fast-paced, adventurous series that I had planned for *Dragon's Gift*. Not to mention the fact that dragons are famous for coveting treasure. Considering where the *deirfiúr* got their skills from, it just made sense to call them treasure hunters.

Even though I write urban fantasy, I strive for accuracy. The *deirfiúr* don't engage in archaeological practices—therefore, I cannot call them archaeologists. I also have a duty as an archaeologist to properly represent my field and our goals—namely, to protect and share history. Treasure hunting doesn't do this. One of the biggest battles that archaeology faces today is protecting cultural heritage from thieves.

I debated long and hard about not only what to call the heroines of this series, but also about how they would do their jobs. I wanted it to involve all the cool things we think about when we think about archaeology—namely, the Indiana Jones stuff, whether it's real or not. But I didn't know quite how to do that while still staying within the bounds of my own ethics. I can cut myself and other writers some slack because this is fiction, but I couldn't go too far into smash and grab treasure hunting.

I consulted some of my archaeology colleagues to get their take, which was immensely helpful. Wayne Lusardi, the State Maritime Archaeologist for Michigan, and Douglas Inglis and Veronica Morris, both archaeologists for Interactive Heritage, were immensely helpful with ideas. My biggest problem was figuring out how to have the heroines steal artifacts from tombs and then sell them and still sleep at night. Everything I've just said is pretty counter to this, right?

That's where the magic comes in. The heroines aren't after the artifacts themselves (they puts them back where they found them, if you recall)—they're after the magic that the artifacts contain. They're more like magic hunters than treasure hunters. That solved a big part of my problem. At least they were putting the artifacts back. Though that's not proper archaeology, I could let it pass. At least it's clear that they believe they shouldn't keep the artifact or harm the site. But the SuperNerd in me said, "Well, that magic is part of the artifact's context. It's important to the artifact and shouldn't be removed and sold."

Now *that* was a problem. I couldn't escape my SuperNerd self, so I was in a real conundrum. Fortunately, that's where the immensely intelligent Wayne Lusardi came in. He suggested that the magic could have an expiration date. If the magic wasn't used before it decayed, it could cause huge problems. Think explosions and tornado spells run amok. It could ruin the entire site, not to mention possibly cause injury and death. That would be very bad.

So now you see why Del and her *deirfiúr* don't just steal artifacts to sell them. Not only is selling the magic cooler, it's also better from an ethical standpoint, especially if the magic was going to cause problems in the long run. These aren't perfect solutions—the perfect solution would be sending in a team of archaeologists to carefully record the site and remove the dangerous magic—but that wouldn't be a very fun book.

Thanks again for reading (especially if you got this far in my ramblings). I hope you enjoyed the story and will stick with Del on the rest of her adventure!

ACKNOWLEDGMENTS

Thank you, Ben, for everything you've done to support me in this career. None of it would be possible without you.

Thank you to Jena O'Connor and Lindsey Loucks for various forms of editing. The book is immensely better because of you! And thank you to Rebecca Frank for the beautiful cover. You really bring Del to life.

Thank you to Tami Mcclain for providing the excellent name for the band on Connor's T-shirt—Peatbog Faeries. They're even a real band!

Thank you so much to the kind folks who did some early reading on this book to make sure I made sense. Seirra Page, Annette Geiger, Kimberly Minnick, and Sarah Leenart—I really appreciate your help. And thank you to all the other awesome folks who volunteered.

The Dragon's Gift series is a product of my two lives: one as an archaeologist and one as a novelist. Combining these two took a bit of work. I'd like to thank my friends, Wayne Lusardi, the State Maritime Archaeologist for Michigan, and Douglas Inglis and Veronica Morris, both archaeologists for Interactive Heritage, for their ideas about how to have a treasure hunter heroine that doesn't conflict too much with archaeology's ethics. The Author's Note contains a bit more about this if you are interested.

And last but certainly not least, thank you to all of my awesome readers! You guys make this all possible and I can't begin to tell you how much I appreciate your support.

GLOSSARY

Alpha Council - There are two governments that enforce law for supernaturals—the Alpha Council and the Order of the Magica. The Alpha Council governs all shifters. They work cooperatively with Alpha Council when necessary - for example, when capturing FireSouls.

Blood Sorceress - A type of Magica who can create magic using blood.

Conjurer - A Magica who uses magic to create something from nothing. They cannot create magic, but if there is magic around them, they can put that magic into their conjuration.

Cŵn Annwn – Spectral hounds of the Welsh Underworld.

Dark Magic - The kind that is meant to harm. It's not necessarily bad, but it often is.

Deirfiúr - Sisters in Irish.

Demons - Often employed to do evil. They live in various hells but can be released upon the earth if you know how to get to them and then get them out. If they are killed on Earth, they are sent back to their hell.

Dragon Sense - A FireSoul's ability to find treasure. It is an internal sense that pulls them toward what they seek. It is easiest to find gold, but they can find anything or anyone that is valued by someone.

Elemental Mage – A rare type of mage who can manipulate all of the elements.

Enchanted Artifacts – Artifacts can be imbued with magic that lasts after the death of the person who put the magic into the artifact (unlike a spell that has not been put into an artifact—these spells disappear after the Magica's death). But magic is not stable. After a period of time—hundreds or thousands of years depending on the circumstance—the magic will degrade. Eventually, it can go bad and cause many problems.

Fire Mage – A mage who can control fire.

FireSoul - A very rare type of Magica who shares a piece of the dragon's soul. They can locate treasure and steal the gifts (powers) of other supernaturals. With practice, they can manipulate the gifts they steal, becoming the strongest of that gift. They are despised and feared. If they are caught, they are thrown in the Prison of Magical Deviants.

The Great Peace - The most powerful piece of magic ever created. It hides magic from the eyes of humans.

Hearth Witch – A Magica who is versed in magic relating to hearth and home. They are often good at potions and protective spells and are also very perceptive when on their own turf.

Magica - Any supernatural who has the power to create magic—witches, sorcerers, mages. All are governed by the Order of the Magica.

Mirror Mage - A Magica who can temporarily borrow the powers of other supernaturals. They can mimic the powers as long as they are near the other supernatural. Or they can hold on to the power, but once they are away from the other supernatural, they can only use it once.

The Origin - The descendent of the original alpha shifter. They are the most powerful shifter and can turn into any species.

Order of the Magica - There are two governments that enforce law for supernaturals—the Alpha Council and the Order of the Magica. The Order of the Magica govern all Magica. They work cooperatively with the Alpha Council when necessary - for example, when capturing FireSouls.

Phantom - A type of supernatural that is similar to a ghost. They are incorporeal. They feed off the misery and pain of others, forcing them to relive their greatest nightmares and fears. They do not have a fully functioning mind like a human or supernatural. Rather, they are a shadow of their former selves. Half bloods are extraordinarily rare.

Seeker - A type of supernatural who can find things. FireSouls often pass off their dragon sense as Seeker power.

Shifter - A supernatural who can turn into an animal. All are governed by the Alpha Council.

Transporter - A type of supernatural who can travel anywhere. Their power is limited and must regenerate after each use.

Warden of the Underworld - A one of a kind position created by Roarke. He keeps order in the Underworld.

ABOUT LINSEY

Before becoming a writer, Linsey Hall was a nautical archaeologist who studied shipwrecks from Hawaii and the Yukon to the UK and the Mediterranean. She credits fantasy and historical romances with her love of history and her career as an archaeologist. After a decade of tromping around the globe in search of old bits of stuff that people left lying about, she settled down and started penning her own romance novels. Her Dragon's Gift series draws upon her love of history and the paranormal elements that she can't help but include.

Copyright 2017 by Linsey Hall
Published by Bonnie Doon Press Inc.

Linsey@LinseyHall.com
www.LinseyHall.com
https://twitter.com/HiLinseyHall
https://www.facebook.com/LinseyHallAuthor

BONNIE
DOON
PRESS

ISBN 978-1-942085-24-9